D0871761

A Deadly Chapter

Jan Fields

AnniesFiction.com

Library of Congress-in-Publication Data
A Deadly Chapter / by Jan Fields
p. cm.
I. Title
2017939683

AnniesFiction.com
(800) 282-6643
Secrets of the Castleton Manor Library™
Series Creator: Shari Lohner
Series Editors: Jane Haertel and Janice Tate
Cover Illustrator: Jesse Reisch

10 11 12 13 14 | Printed in China | 9 8 7 6 5 4 3 2 1

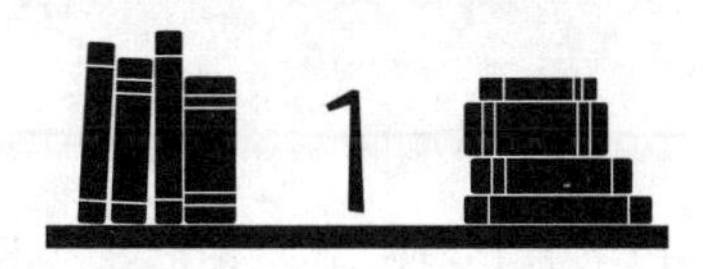

"Darkness is cheap, and Scrooge liked it." Spoken in a deep rolling baritone, the words rumbled through the group that stood in front of the crackling fireplace in the two-story library. The speaker paused and silence filled the room, disturbed only by the soft rustle of taffeta and the snap of the fire. Nearly everyone standing in the Castleton Manor library wore Victorian garb in shades of brown, magenta, and black. Faith Newberry suspected this group didn't miss too many chances to trot out their Victorian finery, but she definitely felt underdressed as she stood among the Charles Dickens Society members during the dramatic reading.

As librarian of the beautiful Castleton Manor library, Faith was required to attend the reading, but it was no hardship. She'd always loved Dickens and could recite much of *A Christmas Carol* by heart. The story had been a family favorite when she was a child, and she'd seen nearly every movie adaptation ever made, even the animated ones. With its air of history, the magnificent library at Castleton Manor was a perfect venue for the reading. With its massively high ceiling, the space was large enough to create a slight echo as the story was read, which added to the spooky quality.

Built in 1895 and filled with craftsmanship and furniture that fit its French Renaissance chateau style, Castleton Manor was anything but spooky, but it did have character. And the library reflected that character. A carved walnut ceiling topped a room that was a perfect marriage of craftsmanship and artistry.

The library housed literally thousands of volumes but still had more than enough room to host a dramatic reading in front of the huge fireplace. The red velvet furniture that normally circled the fireplace had been moved back to allow room for both the readers and the audience to stand through the performance. Faith suspected sitting would be difficult in some of the fancy taffeta gowns.

As with all the public rooms in the manor, the library had a Christmas tree tucked into one corner, if an eleven-foot tree could be tucked. The sparkling white lights and assorted red ornaments added a touch of whimsy to the room. Evergreen boughs wrapped around lamps and draped across the fireplace mantel lent a lovely scent to the air. No one could doubt that it was Christmas at Castleton Manor.

The deep voice picked up the story again. "But before he shut his heavy door, he walked through his rooms to see that all was right. He had just enough recollection of the face to desire to do that." The reader, Charles Huffam, clearly loved the sound of his own voice. His pleasure at the attention of every member of the Charles Dickens Society had pinked his normally pale cheeks. He wore fawn-colored pants, a heavily embroidered waistcoat, and a jacket that was a shade lighter than the pants. In one hand, he carried a shining black walking stick with a silver handle, and in the other, a top hat.

The clothes were impressive, but it was the man's countenance that impressed Faith the most. With a hooked nose, craggy features, wild curly hair with a receding hairline, and a similarly wild beard and mustache, he looked as if he might have stepped out of an old portrait of Charles Dickens himself. It was really no wonder he was the president of the society.

A younger man stood beside the society president, holding a length of heavy chain and wearing a gloomy expression. At his feet, a shaggy mixed-breed dog stared up at him with rapt attention. The sight of the bright, attentive pet made Faith miss Watson, her mischievous tuxedo cat. She'd left him behind at the cottage for his own good since she knew there would be dogs in attendance and Watson loved to tease dogs.

Castleton Manor welcomed pets and encouraged guests to bring them along to the public rooms. It was one of the things Faith most appreciated about the job, and she usually brought Watson to work with her. She might as well bring him, as Watson had an uncanny ability to turn up even when she'd pointedly left him behind.

The ornately printed card resting on an artist easel near the fireplace identified the dog's owner as the society's vice president, Walden Garder. Faith would have guessed Mr. Garder's age to be late thirties, right around her own. His long, lean build was accentuated by a full-length black wool coat trimmed in ratty fur, along with fingerless gloves and a ragged gray scarf. When he had read Bob Cratchit's lines, the scarf was drawn around his neck, but now he had it looped around his head in preparation for the portrayal of Marley's ghost. In both hands, he clutched a length of heavy chain.

Charles's voice dropped to a hoarse stage whisper. "The bells ceased as they had begun, together. They were succeeded by a clanking noise, deep down below, as if some person were dragging a heavy chain over the casks in the wine-merchant's cellar." Charles paused and Walden rattled his chain. "Scrooge then remembered to have heard that ghosts in haunted houses were described as dragging chains." Another rattle.

Faith shivered as she hung on every word of the familiar story. Then Walden gestured to the dog at his feet. The eager animal lifted his nose to the air and howled, a long, mournful sound that went perfectly with the story.

As Walden began reciting Jacob Marley's lines, Faith glanced around at the audience. She had taken most of the day off and had spent it in town Christmas shopping, so she hadn't been at the manor when the society checked in this morning. As she took in the group around her, she saw two or three other people in everyday clothes and felt a little less conspicuous in her black gored skirt and deep burgundy sweater. At least her color choices fit in.

Charles's stentorian voice pulled her attention back to the speakers. "At this the spirit raised a frightful cry, and shook its chain with such a dismal and appalling noise, that Scrooge held on tight to his chair, to save himself from falling in a swoon." Walden rattled his chain, and his dog howled dismally.

"But how much greater was his horror, when the phantom taking off the bandage round its head, as if it were too warm to wear indoors," Charles said, drawing the words out for dramatic effect, "its lower jaw dropped down upon its breast!"

His booming voice made Faith jump, and the smattering of nervous giggles around her led her to believe she wasn't the only one to react that way. She leaned over to whisper to the woman beside her, "He has an amazing voice."

"I suppose," the woman said, her own voice thick with a French accent. The response was so unexpected that Faith turned to look at the woman more closely. She couldn't have been there long, or Faith would have noticed her earlier. Unlike the other society members in their Victorian finery, her dark slacks and thin, black sweater were nondescript.

As Jacob Marley explained to Scrooge about the pending visitation of the three Christmas ghosts, Faith knew the reading was nearly finished for the night. The society planned dramatic readings throughout the weeklong gala that included panel discussions on everything from Victorian medicine to Victorian politics. They even had a morning set aside for playing Victorian parlor games. The whole gala ended on a high point with a lavish Victorian ball complete with a live orchestra for the dancing.

The morning after the ball, the manor would close down for Christmas, and Faith would head home for the first time since she'd started the job. She was looking forward to seeing her family. With a smile, she mused that her Christmas shopping earlier in the day had certainly reflected that. She knew she was going to get a scolding for spoiling her young nephew when her sister saw all the gifts.

The readers finished the first night's portion of *A Christmas Carol*, and the audience clapped enthusiastically.

As she clapped, Faith slipped away from the group around the fireplace. People had been shifting position all through the reading, so Faith knew her own retreat from the crowd wouldn't be obvious. Still, she noticed that Marlene Russell, the assistant manager of Castleton Manor, gave her a disapproving look as they passed. Marlene then continued her weaving journey through the crowd to the fireplace and began to give some announcements about the upcoming events.

Once Faith reached a more open area of the library, she felt a rush of relief. She didn't suffer from social anxiety, but the crowd had crept closer to the readers throughout the performance, making the audience denser than she cared for.

Faith managed to reach the refreshment table before the rest of the audience had drifted over. Normally, they didn't serve refreshments in the library, since sticky fingers and vintage books were not a good combination, but the society had made a special request, and Marlene had been unusually agreeable for some reason. Faith suspected the agreeability had come at a fairly steep cost for the society.

As Faith reached the table, she spotted Laura, a young woman whose job description tended to be a bit fluid, as she was shifted from one chore to another around the manor. The constant shifting wasn't because of Laura's preference. Although rather nervous, she was a pleasant, eager person but almost chronically clumsy. Since Faith was already dubious about food in the library, seeing Laura pouring punch into glasses made her distinctly uneasy.

Faith stepped closer to Brooke Milner, the manor's sous-chef, who was overseeing the refreshment table. "Brooke," Faith whispered, "please tell me there is nothing sticky or red among the snacks."

Brooke grinned at Faith, her blue eyes sparkling. "None. This menu has been chosen carefully to be both tasty and stain resistant." She gestured at the filled trays. "Plum pudding bites in pop-in-your-mouth portions to lessen crumbs and sticky fingers, and roasted chestnuts in paper cones, still warm. Plus, we have some foie gras and a delicious mulled cider." She followed Faith's nervous gaze toward Laura. "And the punch glasses are actually fancy plastic."

"Sounds perfectly safe," Faith said, consciously pushing down her unease. "And perfectly delicious. I haven't had chestnuts since I was a little girl. My grandmother loved them."

"They're yummy. We didn't roast them on an open fire, but they came out just right anyway."

"Sampled your own wares?" Faith teased. Brooke loved eating nearly as much as cooking, though her high metabolism and busy lifestyle kept her from looking as if she did. Brooke had been one of the first people at the manor to befriend Faith, and she had quickly grown to be a dear friend, ready to help out whenever needed. Faith had called on Brooke for both food and fashion advice. She also tended to get romantic advice from Brooke, though that came unsolicited.

"A good sous-chef never serves anything she hasn't tasted," Brooke said seriously. Then her face brightened again. "And I aspire to be a very good sous-chef." She peeked over at the group around the fireplace. The two actors beamed as different society members offered compliments on their performance. Faith could hear Charles offering falsely modest remarks as clearly as if the man were standing beside her.

"Do you think Charles Huffam will be coming over here soon?" Brooke asked.

Does she sound eager to meet him? From her observations of the society's boastful president, Faith found she had little interest in talking with him. "I think he's enjoying his accolades right at the moment." At the clear disappointment on Brooke's face, Faith added, "I doubt anyone could resist your delicious food for long. I'm sure he'll be over."

"Good." Brooke rubbed her hands together. "Excellent."

"Why all the enthusiasm?"

Brooke dropped her voice and leaned over the table to whisper, "He's the president of Huffam Publishing."

"And that's a secret?" Faith whispered back.

"No, but Huffam Publishing publishes the most fantastic themed cookbooks. You know the cookbook author retreat we had a couple of months ago?"

Considering that retreat had nearly gotten Faith killed, it stood out in her memory. "I think I can recall it," she said drily.

"Well, I've been thinking about doing a cookbook ever since the retreat. I've collected Victorian recipes into a Dickens-inspired cookbook manuscript. I've tweaked these classic dishes with modern techniques and healthier ingredients. I think it would be perfect for Huffam Publishing."

"You're not going to pitch a book to him at the retreat, are you? If Marlene caught you doing that, she'd blow a gasket." Marlene could be more than a little harsh about staff soliciting any of the guests.

"That's why we're whispering," Brooke said. "I already mentioned it to him. I spoke to him after dinner. He sounded interested. In fact, I practically had to hold him off with one hand while I talked about the cookbook. He told me we'd have to talk about it later. This is later."

"This is dangerous," Faith said. "Marlene is right here."

"I noticed," Brooke grumbled. "You don't suppose she'll leave early, do you?"

"That seems unlikely." Before Faith could say anything else, the first group of society members reached the table, and Brooke turned her attention to describing the snacks.

A tiny white-haired woman in black taffeta with a high lace collar touched Faith's arm. "You're the librarian here, isn't that right?"

Faith turned a warm smile toward the woman. "Yes, my name is Faith Newberry. Is there anything I can help you with?"

"I'm Ethel Linten. I read in the packet that guests can check books out of the library," the woman said, her voice a scratchy near whisper.

"Yes, you can check out any book for the length of your stay. We have an extensive collection of works by Charles Dickens, including some valuable pieces that cannot be loaned, I'm afraid."

"That's all right," the woman said. "I'm actually hoping to check out a mystery. Something gothic and creepy."

"I think I have several you'll like." Faith led the woman toward the narrow bookcases near the library doorway. She'd gathered many of the most popular mysteries together into that easy-to-access location, since mysteries were the ones guests seemed to ask for the most. Faith couldn't blame them, as she loved an interesting puzzle in a spooky setting herself. They'd nearly reached the bookcases when a handsome older woman in a dark green dress opened the door, her gaze darting around the library.

The woman staggered into the room and shouted, "I've been robbed!"

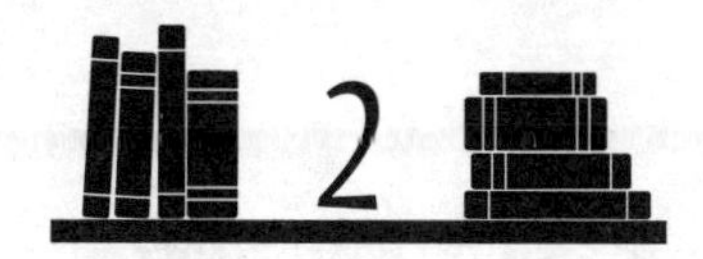

2

Faith hurried to catch the trembling woman by the arm as everyone in the room headed toward them. "Are you all right?"

"I'm fine," she snapped, pulling her arm free from Faith's hand. "But my jewelry is gone from my room. Every piece. What kind of place is this?"

Marlene joined Faith at the woman's side. "Don't worry," she said. "I just called the police and they are on their way. I assure you, this is not something we have experienced at Castleton Manor before."

Faith noticed that Marlene wisely left out references to *other* problems Castleton Manor had experienced.

"Did you see the person who robbed you?" Marlene continued.

"How would I have managed that?" The woman's temper was short, but at least her anger seemed to steady her and she was no longer shaking. She straightened up and looked down her nose at Marlene. "I was down here listening to that nincompoop drone on until I couldn't bear it anymore. Did you know his first name is actually John, and he goes by his middle name to increase his similarity to Dickens? The very idea of him being anything like Dickens! Anyway, I returned to my room and found it robbed. Every piece of my jewelry is gone. Dora and Nell are so traumatized I can't even get them out from under the bed."

"Dora and Nell?" Faith echoed.

The woman turned toward her. "My darling cats." Her attention snapped back to Marlene. "I will expect this establishment to pay for my lost items."

As Marlene protested, Faith started to back away. She really didn't know anything about the manor's culpability in that kind of situation, and it appeared the woman was physically fine. She'd barely moved when the upset guest pushed past Marlene and snatched Faith's wrist. "Don't go. You have a sensible look about you. Stay." When Faith gaped in alarm at the woman's tight grasp on her arm, the guest's expression softened. "Please."

Faith patted the woman's hand gently, despite the fact that her grip was borderline painful. "I'll stay. I'm Faith Newberry, the librarian here. And you are . . . ?"

"Evelyn Pugh," the woman said, her tone softening. She glared pointedly at Marlene. "Who are you?"

Marlene bristled at the woman's tone but made a visible effort to respond pleasantly—or pleasantly for Marlene, anyway. "I'm Marlene Russell, the assistant manager at Castleton Manor. I assure you, everything possible will be done to recover your valuables. The Lighthouse Bay police are efficient and effective. Though, really, Mrs. Pugh, you should have let us lock your jewelry in the safe in our security office if the pieces are truly valuable."

The woman waved off the idea. "I don't care to run up and down the stairs every time I want to wear a piece of my own jewelry."

"Do you have a list of the stolen items, Mrs. Pugh?" Faith asked.

"Please call me Evelyn. And yes, of course. The jewelry is all insured, though much of it couldn't really be replaced if I tried." The woman had some nerve, or perhaps she was just upset. If the jewelry was insured, Evelyn couldn't actually expect the manor to reimburse her for her losses.

Evelyn sighed deeply. "I should go back up to my room. My poor darlings are in such a state. I hate to leave them alone. Faith, would you be willing to join me?" She gave Marlene another haughty stare. "You may send up the police when they arrive. I am in the Jane Austen Suite."

"Actually, Evelyn, *I* should come with you," Marlene said, smiling tightly. "Faith needs to be down here attending to the guests at the reading. The library is her job."

"*You* may call me Mrs. Pugh," Evelyn replied sharply. "And very well. I suppose my little missing-irreplaceable-jewelry problem shouldn't take priority over grown men playacting." She nearly spat the last word. "Come along if you must, Ms. Russell." She turned on her heel and marched out of the library.

Marlene glared at the woman's retreating back, then took a deep breath before turning to Faith. "Report this to security, and send up the police when they arrive. In the meanwhile, try to defuse worry in the other guests."

As Marlene stormed after Evelyn, Faith turned to gaze back into the library. She saw that most of the guests stood nearby, listening intently. "I'm certain everything will be fine," she said. "Let's enjoy the delicious refreshments."

"Should we go and check on our rooms?" one woman asked.

"You are free to go wherever you like," Faith said with a smile. "But it might be best to wait for the police to arrive and get their advice."

At that, most of the people turned back toward the refreshment table, though Charles remained. "I hope you will not allow the police to make a nuisance of themselves. I see no reason for them to bother any of the society members. Surely questioning your staff will be sufficient. It must have been one of them."

Faith felt the edges of her reassuring smile grow tight. "We cannot dictate the terms of a police investigation. The Lighthouse Bay Police Department is very good."

"Don't be such a snob, Charles," Walden said, clapping the bigger man on the back and getting a dirty look in return. "I think it is much more likely that someone in the society robbed the old girl. Everyone knew Evelyn carted around a fortune in Victorian jewelry. She couldn't have been more casual about it."

"The Charles Dickens Society is made up of literary enthusiasts, not jewel thieves," Charles said, his mustache bristling with his indignation. "And I'll thank you to stay out of this, Walden, since you clearly have no idea what you're talking about."

"What *are* you talking about?" This came from an older woman wearing an elaborate red gown full of ruffles and flounces. The woman's hair was dyed coal black and curled in ringlets that seemed suited for a much younger person. She also wore a prodigious amount of makeup, some of which had bled into the wrinkles in her face. "I do hope this gala isn't going to turn into anything ghastly."

Charles cut his eyes toward her. "It certainly won't, Octavia. I wouldn't allow it. We are here to celebrate Dickens and Christmas. As Dickens himself would say, 'Happy, happy Christmas, that can win us back to the delusions of our childish days; that can recall to the old man the pleasures of his youth; that can transport the sailor and the traveller, thousands of miles away, back to his own fire-side and his quiet home!' That is the goal for this gathering and I will not have it disrupted."

"You may not have as much control as you think," Walden said. "Not everyone jumps simply because you tell them to, Charles. As distasteful as you may find it, we all need to help the police in whatever way we can."

"Walden, do stop talking nonsense," the older woman said.

"Are you sure it's nonsense?" This came from a younger woman who had trailed behind Octavia, wearing a much simpler gray-blue dress. She was a softer version of Octavia, making Faith suspect they were mother and daughter.

"Of course it is," Octavia insisted. "Charles is the president of the society, as well as the person who chose this particular venue. For what we're paying for this big, drafty place, I would certainly expect the management to do what he says."

Faith didn't have a clue how to reply to any of that. Though Castleton Manor always tried to ensure the guests had a wonderful time, that wasn't the same thing as letting a guest dictate the literary retreat's policy or tell the police how to behave. And on top of that, as a sixty-thousand-square-foot mansion and one of the premier resorts in the country, Castleton Manor was certainly big and opulent, but it wasn't at all drafty.

Before Faith could come up with some response to the slur against her place of employment, her attention was drawn to the library door when everyone around her quieted and turned in that direction. She recognized Officer Bryan Laddy and almost groaned. It wasn't that Officer Laddy wasn't competent, because he was. He was thorough, smart, and so rigidly by the book that Faith found him intimidating most of the time.

"Miss Newberry," the officer said as he crossed the room. "I understand there has been a robbery."

"Someone broke into the Jane Austen Suite and stole some jewelry. The owner wasn't in the suite at the time." *Thank goodness.*

"Good. That's probably why there were no injuries. Thieves unexpectedly interrupted can turn violent." He peered suspiciously around the library at the guests as if he would recognize the perpetrator. "Was this gathering going on at the time of the robbery or has it formed in response?"

"Everyone was here for a dramatic performance," Faith said. "It seems the robbery occurred while the society members were here in the library listening to the reading."

"*A Christmas Carol,*" Charles announced theatrically. "I was the primary reader. I am Charles Huffam, president of the Charles Dickens Society." He narrowed his eyes. "And I expect you to dispatch this matter with all speed and discretion."

Officer Laddy ignored Charles's command and turned his attention back to Faith. "Is the victim also a society member?"

"She is," Faith said.

"And was she at the reading?"

"Apparently she was at the beginning of the reading but left early to return to her room," Faith said.

"How odd," Octavia remarked. "I cannot imagine walking out while Charles was performing. I found the entire experience riveting." When the officer's gaze settled on her, she drew herself up. "I am Octavia Skimsby, and this is my daughter, Caroline." She gestured vaguely toward the younger woman.

"Members could go and come during the reading. Anyone here could have slipped away to the Jane Austen Suite," the officer mused.

"*I* couldn't have," Charles said. "I was reading, and I imagine the audience would have noticed if I'd marched off to commit burglary. Not that I would ever disrupt the society in such a fashion. As Dickens said, 'Whatever I have tried to do in life, I have tried with all my heart to do well; that whatever I have devoted myself to, I have devoted myself to completely; that in great aims and in small, I have always been thoroughly in earnest.' I have made that my creed."

Officer Laddy blinked at him, clearly trying to sort out how the quote applied to the burglary.

"Walden was here throughout the reading as well," Caroline said, drawing the officer's attention away from his scrutiny of Charles. "And my mother was with me the whole time."

"Very well," Officer Laddy said. "I'll want to speak with each member of the society in addition to any of the staff who may have been in the building, but I'll go up and examine the scene first." He raised his voice to be heard throughout the library. "Please stay in the library until I return. I will have questions for each of you. I will also ask you later to go upstairs and check your own rooms for any missing items. But for the time being, please remain here."

There was a rustle of movement and muttered remarks, but no one headed toward the door.

"Would you like me to show you the way?" Faith asked.

"That's not necessary," Officer Laddy said. "I've been there before." He turned so smartly that he almost looked military and strode out of the library.

Faith forced a smile at the group milling around. "It sounds like we'll have time to enjoy the refreshments."

"I hope that young man isn't going to fixate on the ridiculous theory that a member of the Charles Dickens Society would walk out in the middle of the dramatic reading and rob someone's room," Octavia said. "I have never heard such a preposterous idea in my life."

"Well, Mother," Caroline said, "we know at least one person did walk out in the middle of the reading. Evelyn went back to her room."

The older woman glared at her daughter. "Don't be a ninny, Caroline. Evelyn certainly wouldn't steal her own jewelry."

"That's not what I was suggesting. If Evelyn was willing to leave, then certainly someone motivated by theft would be equally willing to leave. With all due respect for the excellent reading skills of Mr. Huffam and Mr. Garder, I rather suspect the possibility of acquiring over $100,000 worth of jewelry would be quite an enticement."

"How do you know how much Mrs. Pugh's jewelry was worth?" Faith asked.

"Everyone knew," Walden said. "Evelyn was always going on about the stuff. One of the pieces apparently belonged to Queen Victoria herself. At any rate, I doubt there is a member on the roster who didn't know the jewelry was worth a bucketload."

"I still refuse to believe it was a member," Octavia said with a sniff. "It's this dreadful venue." She narrowed her eyes at Faith. "How many maids do you employ here? I bet one of them took it."

"I'm not connected with housekeeping," Faith said. "I'm the librarian. But I know Castleton Manor is quite careful in screening its employees." She nearly winced as she said the last part since there *had* been some issues with past employees, including Marlene Russell herself.

"I have to agree with Octavia," Charles said. "The resort clearly does not properly control its employees. Why, just today I was accosted by one of the waitresses in the dining room. The ridiculous girl wanted to pitch a book! Now, don't get me wrong, she was a pretty little thing and I wouldn't have minded getting to know her a bit." He guffawed at his own crudity. "But thinking I would be interested in her midnight scribblings? How absurd."

"That is nervy," Octavia said. "I hope you reported her. If we don't call those kinds of people to account, there's no telling where it will end." Then she gave a dry laugh. "Well, actually, I suppose we do know where it ends—in the theft of one's jewelry."

"I don't know," Caroline said. "It doesn't seem like such a ridiculous happening. After all, you are a publisher. The woman might simply have thought you'd be interested in book ideas."

"I'm sure it was something like that," Faith added, her stomach clenched in alarm at the idea of Brooke getting in trouble over talking with Charles.

"Was it at least a good book?" Octavia asked.

Charles sneered. "It was written by a waitress or a maid or some such. How could it possibly be worth my time?" He laughed. "As Dickens said, 'There are books of which the backs and covers are by far the best parts.' I don't doubt that her nonsensical collection of recipes would be such a book."

"You should report her," Octavia insisted.

"I intend to," Charles said, "as soon as Marlene is done with the police. I believe I can trust her to handle it and make certain I don't have to deal with that sort of thing in the future. She knows the importance of people staying within their stations. Or at least she did when I knew her."

"How interesting," Caroline said. "Do you know Dickens had a quote for that too? 'May not the complaint, that common people are above their station, often take its rise in the fact of uncommon people being below theirs?'"

"That makes no sense at all," Octavia snapped. "You really shouldn't prattle on, Caroline."

Faith was still focused on the one surprising thing Charles had said. "You know Marlene?"

"I did," he said. "Years ago. She was quite the spitfire when she was young. I must say, she hasn't aged particularly well, but then some don't. Still, I'll talk with her about the whole waitress fiasco."

"You don't need to go to that kind of trouble," Faith assured him. "I know you're very busy with the gala. I would be happy to take care of it for you."

His lips stretched into a wolfish grin. "You would? How kind of you. I thought you said that the housekeeping staff wasn't your responsibility."

"No, but Marlene specifically said I should do whatever was necessary to ensure everyone had a good time during this week," Faith said. She didn't mention that Marlene gave every staff member the same bossy pep talk before every event. "So I can certainly make sure that you are not bothered again with any book propositions."

"That's very nice of you. Certainly you are a fine representative of this place," Charles said, suddenly sliding closer to Faith. To her shock, he took her hand and rubbed his thumb across the backs of her fingers. "As Dickens would say, 'No one is useless in this world who lightens the burdens of another.' Thank you, my dear. Now, do tell me your name again."

"Newberry," she said with a painfully strained smile as she tugged at her trapped fingers. "Faith Newberry. I'm happy to help." She suppressed a shudder as Charles bent and kissed the back of her hand.

Then, over Charles's shoulder, she caught sight of something that made her heart thump in her chest. Brooke had slipped out from behind the table of refreshments and was heading straight for Charles.

"Faith, what are you doing?" The grating voice of Marlene behind her made Faith jump and jerk her hand away from Charles. She turned a panicked glance in Brooke's direction and saw her friend still heading her way. Faith had to do something before Charles caught sight of Brooke and turned her in to Marlene. With Marlene's stress over the burglary, Faith knew there was only one way that could end—with Brooke losing her job.

3

Brooke stopped about five feet behind Charles, apparently either noticing Faith's expression of utter terror or not wanting to say anything in front of Marlene. Whichever it was, Faith felt a wave of relief. Now all she had to do was keep Charles and Brooke apart until she had a chance to warn her friend. Faith raised a hand to her hair and used the motion to cover as she shook her head and waved Brooke away.

Her friend frowned in confusion but backed up. She mouthed, "What?"

"Later," Faith mouthed back.

"Miss Newberry," Charles said, jerking Faith's attention back to him by reaching for her hand again. "Are you all right?"

"Yes, I'm sorry," Faith said, easing her hand away. "It's been a tense evening. Please excuse me." She turned to walk over to Marlene, who stood waiting for Faith's response to her question. "You wanted to speak to me?"

"If you can stop flirting with the guests and listen to me," Marlene hissed as she caught hold of Faith's arm and towed her farther away from the group. "Wolfe is with Officer Laddy and will be down directly. I need to make some phone calls. Are you going to be able to handle things here without resorting to overfamiliarity with our guests?"

"Yes," Faith said, trying not to sound too eager since that would be sure to set off Marlene's suspicion meter, but Faith needed her to leave before Charles decided to go ahead and complain about Brooke. "Everyone seems to be enjoying the refreshments. There are concerns about the burglary, but no one is panicking."

"Good," Marlene said. "This is a nightmare."

Faith personally thought they'd weathered worse things since she'd come to work at Castleton Manor. "I'm sure the police will soon find who broke into the room."

Marlene rolled her eyes. "Actually I expect they'll get in the way and disrupt the flow of operations, but they're a necessary evil. I'm heading up again. Watch for Mr. Jaxon."

"I will."

"And stop flirting."

"I wasn't flirting." Faith's protest was directed to Marlene's back as the assistant manager had already spun and rushed away.

"Is that your boss?"

Faith turned to face Caroline, who had crept up behind her. "Yes."

"She reminds me of my mother." Caroline offered Faith her hand. "I'm Caroline Skimsby, and you are Faith Newberry, librarian." She waved a hand in the direction of the impossibly tall bookcases around the room. "This is a magnificent library. You must love working in it."

Faith shared a warm handshake with the young woman and brightened at the return to her favorite topic. "Yes, I'm incredibly blessed to work here."

"I'm so excited about your presentation tomorrow. It was one of the first things I circled on my agenda," Caroline said. "My mother and I have a few vintage books, mostly Dickens, as you'd imagine, though I also collect poetry. I can't wait to learn more on how to care for them properly. I've found some information online, but that's not the same as learning from an expert. Then I might feel more comfortable expanding my collection. I would hate to destroy something so valuable through ignorance."

"You're very kind," Faith said. "By the way, we have an extensive poetry collection here in the library if you're interested in it. You're welcome to check some out to read while you're here. We keep a lot of the great poets, as well as some unique collections."

"I'd like that. I found a delightful book of mystery-themed poetry in one of the bookcases in our suite. I've been enjoying it tremendously. I believe I'll have to track down a copy for my own—*eek!*" Caroline jumped as Charles came up behind her and slipped an arm around her waist.

"What are the two prettiest girls in the room talking about?" he asked.

"Just girl talk," Caroline said as she shifted away from his arm, her tone almost dripping with sarcasm. "We were just comparing froufrou and gewgaws. You know, the sort of simple things girls chat about."

"Ah, the mystery of female beauty," Charles said. It was clear that Caroline's sarcasm flew right over his head. "Miss Havisham would be proud. 'Break their hearts my pride and hope, break their hearts and have no mercy!' And so goes the rapier of your beauty right into my heart."

"Actually our conversation wasn't nearly so mysterious. We were talking about the books in the library," Faith said, "which I was saying are available for reading by society members throughout their stay."

Charles shook his head. "I brought my own reading. I cannot imagine trying to wade through the jumbled collection in here. I took a look at the books on the shelves in my suite and found them an outlandish and haphazard mess."

Faith felt her temper rise. The book collection in each suite was eclectic by design so there was sure to be something for every reader. She would hardly typify any of them as a *mess*. She had spent hours organizing and sorting books into the perfect arrangements.

From the corner of her eye, Faith saw someone appear beside her and then heard the deep, warm voice of Wolfe Jaxon. "Our collection here is very well maintained. Faith can help you pick a book for any interest. She's an amazing librarian."

Faith felt a warm glow at her boss's praise. The Jaxon family owned Castleton Manor, as well as a number of other properties and businesses. Wolfe handled the running of many of them. His apartment was on the third floor of the mansion. In fact, it was the entire third floor.

Faith introduced Wolfe to Caroline and Charles. "Mr. Huffam is the president of the Charles Dickens Society," she explained.

Wolfe thrust out his hand to shake with Charles, who eyed him with displeasure. "So this is your family home? Must be nice."

"It is amazing," Wolfe admitted. "And we're glad to have the opportunity to share it with our guests. I live here myself when I'm in the area." He smiled at Faith. "I hate to steal you from our guests, but may I borrow you? I won't keep you long."

Faith excused herself to Caroline and Charles. At first Caroline looked stricken at being left with Charles, but Faith saw Octavia approaching and assumed Caroline wouldn't be alone with the unpleasant man for long.

"The burglary is such a horrible thing," Faith said to Wolfe as they made their way to a fairly empty spot near the antique globe. "Mrs. Pugh was very upset."

"She calmed down quickly," Wolfe said. "Laddy has that effect on people when he tries. I think it's the way he radiates efficiency and competence. And to be completely honest, she seemed much more worried about her cats than her jewels."

"Now if Officer Laddy will just solve this."

Wolfe sighed. "That may be easier said than done. There weren't many clues, though Laddy found fine scratches around the lock, which suggested it was picked."

"That surely proves it wasn't the housekeeping staff. They all have access to master keys and wouldn't need to force the door," Faith said.

"It does suggest that. I believe I will leave it in the able hands of the police." Wolfe rubbed his temples. "You know, now more than ever, I can't wait for a nice quiet holiday when the Dickens Society gala is over. How about you? Are you going home?"

Faith nodded. "To my parents' house in Springfield. I haven't been home since I started work here, so it's going to be especially nice. And it sounds like there will be a lot of family there this year."

"Now I feel terribly guilty," Wolfe said. "Surely we give you some time off now and then."

"I have plenty of time off," Faith assured him. "I have no complaints. I've just been busy settling into the job."

"But you had some time over Thanksgiving?" he said.

Faith was touched by his concern. "I did, but my mother and father went on a Thanksgiving cruise, so I had Thanksgiving here in Lighthouse Bay with my aunt Eileen and my cousin's family. I'm being treated very well here. This is the best job I've ever had, and the benefits are more than adequate."

"Good," he said. His smile warmed his blue-gray eyes. "We don't want to lose you."

"No worries there." She gazed at him curiously. "You know, I thought someone told me your family was planning to spend Christmas in Europe. I was a little surprised to hear you're still here."

"I intend to join them," he said. "But I had some last-minute business in town, so I thought I would take in some of the Lighthouse Bay festivities. I attended the caroling contest last night, and that was quite enjoyable. Did you go?"

"No, I had a quiet evening with Watson after a full day of Christmas shopping. I did a little more shopping this morning, and now I'm almost done."

"That's impressive. You really should catch the tree lighting in town, though. It's the day after tomorrow. The tree lighting was one event my family never missed when I was a child. Say, would you like to go with me? The high school carolers sing and the mayor has a speech, but the best part is when they light the tree. It's magical."

"I'm astonished you can be impressed by one more Christmas tree," Faith said, "considering how many you have here at the manor."

He chuckled. "We do seem almost forest-like, don't we? But the tree in the center of town is fifty feet tall. Even the tree in the Great Hall cannot compete with that. Please come with me. It will be fun to see it through fresh eyes."

"Sure," she said, trying to cover her surprise at the request. "I would like that."

"Excellent." Wolfe glanced toward the door. "There's Officer Laddy now. Excuse me."

Faith watched him cross the room to intercept the police officer, her head spinning. *Did I just accept a date with my boss?* No, surely not. They were friends. It was a friendly invitation, the same as if she were going with Midge or Brooke. *Brooke!* Faith nearly squeaked as she remembered her friend. She had to speak with her before Brooke could talk to Charles again.

Faith scoured the room and spotted Brooke coming out from behind the refreshment table. Faith wove quickly through the crowd and caught her friend in the middle of the room. "I need to talk to you," she whispered.

Brooke raised her eyebrows and gave Faith a sly grin. "Yes, I saw you chatting with Wolfe. Did he finally ask you out?"

"No." Faith paused. "Yes. Maybe. I don't know. That's not what I need to talk to you about."

"Where did he ask you to go?" Brooke asked, eyes sparkling. The younger woman was tenacious when it came to matchmaking and romance.

"The tree lighting, but this is serious. You can't talk to Charles about your book anymore." Faith explained what Charles had said about the encounter, including the fact that Charles and Marlene had known each other in the past. "Right now, he doesn't seem to really remember you and thinks you were a waitress, so you might be all right even if he does talk to Marlene, but it would be best to avoid direct contact with him."

Brooke's expression sharpened. "He thought I was a waitress?"

"Brooke, what's important is that he wanted to complain to Marlene about you. I offered to handle it for him, so I think you're all right, but don't mention the book to him again. He definitely isn't interested, and you'll end up in trouble for sure."

Brooke's cheeks flushed. "I can't believe the nerve of that man. I couldn't have taken even a full minute of his time. What a horrible person. He should be boiled with his own pudding and buried with a stake of holly through his heart!"

Faith almost smiled at the reference to *A Christmas Carol*. She slipped her arm through Brooke's to lead her back toward the refreshment table and away from trouble. "He doesn't deserve your book."

"You can say that again. I wouldn't sell it to him if he begged." Her gaze landed on the frantic woman behind the refreshment table. "Oops, I've been gone too long. Laura is looking overwhelmed."

Faith let go of Brooke's arm and watched as her friend returned to offering treats to the guests. Brooke's bright and happy face gave no sign of how annoyed she was by Charles's crass behavior.

With Brooke safely back on the refreshments, Faith scanned the crowd, wondering if she should keep Charles away from the snacks. As self-absorbed as the man seemed to be, he probably wouldn't notice Brooke, but in her present mood, Faith's friend might do something especially noticeable like spill cider on him. Accidentally, of course.

She caught sight of the publisher near the fireplace. He appeared to be having an intense discussion with the unfriendly Frenchwoman in the black sweater and slacks to whom Faith had spoken earlier. The expression on the woman's face was even more hostile than the one she'd given Faith.

Faith almost smiled. After the horrible things Charles had said about Brooke, she hoped whatever the strange woman was telling him would ruin his whole night. Faith's gaze swept the room again, and she saw Marlene Russell had joined Wolfe and Officer Laddy near the library door. Apparently the officer was finished with his investigation upstairs.

With both her bosses in the library and handling the situation, Faith wondered if it would be a good time to slip away and go home. She'd had a long day and wanted to put her feet up with a cat on her lap. Plus, it wouldn't be a bad idea to get to bed early since she had to give her talk on preserving vintage books after breakfast at the manor tomorrow.

Just to be certain, Faith joined the small group to get permission to leave from Officer Laddy before heading home. Since she hadn't noticed any comings and goings during the reading and didn't know the victim, the police officer bid her good night.

"Have a good evening," Wolfe said. "And thank you again for agreeing to join me for the tree lighting."

Marlene stared from Wolfe to Faith and her scowl sharpened. "You hurry on home," she said, her voice dripping with false concern. "You should get some sleep. You look pale and tired."

"I don't like the idea of you walking by yourself after the burglary," Wolfe said. "If you don't mind waiting, I can walk you."

"Faith will be fine," Marlene insisted. "The burglar is hardly wandering the gardens hoping for someone to rob." She flapped a hand at Faith. "Go on now."

"I really will be fine," Faith assured Wolfe. "I would like to go on home."

"Yes, you look dead on your feet," Marlene said, clearly glad to be getting her way.

I can always count on Marlene to lift my spirits, Faith thought as she thanked Marlene for her concern and slipped out of the library.

The heels of her boots echoed on the marble floor of the long, two-story gallery, which was a favorite of many guests as it offered a spectacular view of the ocean through French doors that opened onto the loggia. The two grand main staircases rose from opposite corners of this room to the landing and from there continued in twin flights sweeping upward in graceful curves to the second floor. The large gallery was sometimes used for special events. In fact, a vendor fair was scheduled for later in the week.

Currently the usual urns of flowers and ferns—scattered throughout to keep the huge space open and welcoming—had been filled with gorgeous Christmas arrangements. Sparkling Christmas trees circled the statue of Agatha Christie and lit up every empty corner. Every surface seemed to be draped with ribbons and greenery, and the scent of pine forest engulfed Faith as she walked. The manor was a gilded work of art that stopped just short of being gaudy.

Once outside in the shadowy darkness, Faith turned up the collar of her long wool coat and wrapped her scarf around the lower part of her face. Somehow her chin and ears always seemed to feel the cold the most, especially with the chill breeze blowing in from the ocean.

The ground crunched under Faith's feet as she broke through the thin layer of snow. They hadn't had much snow yet, which was normal enough for New England. They'd really be buried in January and February. The weather report even predicted warmer days later in the week, though the night air was anything but warm as Faith flexed her freezing fingers inside her gloves.

The path through the gardens was well lit for the most part, even though few guests would be likely to spend much time outside for the next couple of months, especially at night. Later in the week, there would be carriage rides into town, and she knew the manor would offer blankets to help with the chill. Faith had considered going along on the rides, but now that she was just walking in the cold, she wasn't sure the idea was that appealing. *Maybe if Wolfe was there . . .* At the thought, her cheeks warmed even in the bitter wind.

She gave herself a mental shake before her imagination could wander down that road. She and Wolfe were friends, and that was where it would be best to stay, especially because he was her boss. He was also a wealthy and important man. She was a librarian. She had no illusions about her own place in society. She definitely wouldn't fit in with the Jaxons.

"What is wrong with me?" she grumbled, pulling her thoughts away from Wolfe and picking up her pace. *It's the temperature. I read something about that. Hallucinations and crazy thoughts can be caused by cold.*

She'd reached the end of the formal gardens, and the path grew much more shadowed as the distance between lights was longer. She had enough light to avoid running into one of the trees that dotted the path but not nearly as much as when she was in the gardens. The darkness seemed to make the cold more intense.

Then, as Faith walked under a skeletal crab apple tree, she heard a creepy yowl, which immediately reminded her of the unearthly sounds Walden's dog had made during the reading. Faith stopped and looked around, squinting as if that would help her vision penetrate the darkness. Where had the sound come from?

Before she could decide, something dropped out of the tree and landed directly on Faith's shoulder. Something like a needle pierced her neck. She screamed.

4

Faith immediately felt ridiculous about the scream as Watson slithered from her shoulder to the front of her coat where he tried to burrow inside where it was warm. "You nearly gave me a heart attack," she scolded while unbuttoning the top of her coat so she could cuddle her chilly pet. "What were you doing out here anyway? I know I left you snug and warm in the cottage."

Watson had no response, though Faith could feel the faint vibrations of his purring against her throat as he snuggled up against her. "You're lucky you're cute," she said as she rubbed the top of his head with one finger. "Because your nose is cold."

The rest of the walk to the cottage was uneventful, and Faith made a concentrated effort to put the day behind her as she laid a fire in the cottage's small fireplace and cuddled up in her most comfortable chair with a cup of tea on the side table, a book in her hand, and Watson in her lap. She gazed into the dancing flames and thought how life was as perfect as she could imagine.

The next morning dawned even colder than the last, and Faith tucked Watson into her coat again for the walk to the manor. "There's no point pretending you'll stay home just because I leave you there," she grumbled at the purring cat.

Before she headed to the library, she first walked to the manor's gift and coffee shop with Watson trotting along at her heels. Iris Alden stood fussing over a display of Victorian Christmas ornaments. As a retired museum conservator who specialized in caring for early American decorative art, the gift shop manager was more than a little overqualified for her job, but it was clear that she loved it.

"Was someone messing with your display again?" Faith asked.

"If by 'someone' you mean Marlene Russell, yes," Iris said. She put her hands on her hips. "Sometimes I wonder if Marlene has too much time on her hands."

"I think she just likes to be involved," Faith said.

Iris gave her a dubious frown. "You're entirely too kindhearted, Faith." She brushed off her hands, though Faith knew Iris would never allow a speck of dust in her sparkling gift shop. "Coffee?"

"Please."

Watson rubbed against Iris's ankles and she smiled down at him. "You're purring up the wrong tree, you little charmer. I'm out of treats until Midge stops by with a delivery."

Faith's friend Midge Foster was both the concierge veterinarian for Castleton Manor and the owner and baker for Happy Tails Gourmet Bakery. She also supplied a small selection of pet treats for the gift shop and the pet spa. The manor believed in spoiling all their guests, whether two-legged or four-legged.

After collecting a cup of coffee, Faith opened the library for the day. All traces of the refreshments and reading from the night before were gone. The room smelled of pine and high-quality wood cleaner—an almost sweet, waxy smell. Faith walked through the room, carrying Watson as she glanced over the tables, shelves, and floor, just to be certain the cleaning staff hadn't overlooked a crumpled napkin or a discarded treat. Unsurprisingly she didn't find anything like that, though she did reshelve a few books that had clearly been examined and left on the library tables the night before. The cleaning staff never reshelved books, which was exactly as Faith preferred it.

Since she needed to prepare for her presentation on book preservation, Faith settled Watson in one of his favorite spots near the fireplace and pulled on a pair of soft cotton gloves. She carefully took a few books out of their glass display cases and placed them on a table so she could reference them during her talk. Although she'd given many talks and presentations in all sorts of situations, she still preferred not to use a podium—it always felt a little pretentious to her.

As she set up, guests wandered in, and Faith stopped to greet each person. Without their elaborate Victorian finery, they seemed so normal that Faith found it mildly surprising. Most were interested in the Dickens collection, but more than one made a beeline for the mysteries, apparently intent on puzzle solving during the downtime at the gala.

By the time the clock struck ten, she had a full house. To her relief, Charles seemed fixated on Octavia and Caroline, so Faith was spared his off-putting attention. Her audience quieted and turned their faces to her.

Faith beamed at the assembled group, took a deep breath, and began her presentation. "The first thing to remember about vintage books is that they have likes and dislikes just like any of us." And with that, she launched into one of her favorite topics.

Though most of the group before her listened attentively, some even taking notes, Faith had an odd feeling that she was watching some subtle silent movie or maybe a Victorian pantomime. Even without hearing anyone speak, some things were obvious. Octavia batted her eyes at Charles, who gave her a half-hearted smile before directing his stare over the older woman's head to watch her daughter. *Good luck with that*, Faith thought. It was obvious to her that Caroline did not care for Charles's attention at all.

As her gaze swept over the audience, she saw that Caroline wasn't the only one who apparently didn't like Charles. The attractive Frenchwoman who'd spoken with her the night before was glancing frequently in his direction, and if looks could kill, Charles would have keeled over right where he sat. Who was this mysterious woman?

Faith made an effort to pull her attention away from Charles and the women who fixated on him, and she hunted for an attentive face to direct comments toward. She found it helped her focus and energy during a presentation if she made eye contact with people who seemed to be enjoying the talk. Evelyn leaned forward in her chair and smiled encouragement when Faith's eyes met hers.

"Mold loves paper," Faith said. "So it's key to create an environment that discourages mold growth." She explained about the placement of the display cases in the library and how the locations were carefully chosen to keep the books away from the direct sunlight of the terrace doors. "As beautiful as the view outside is, our books don't care for it."

When she finished her presentation, the applause was quiet but sincere, and Faith felt good about her talk. She hadn't stammered or forgotten anything, which she always worried about, even after all the public speaking she'd done.

As she carried the books from her presentation back to their climate-controlled glass cases, Charles met her and tried to take her hands until Faith pulled back. "I'm sorry," she said. "Let me get these books put away safely."

"By all means," he boomed. "That was a brilliant presentation. I certainly enjoy useful information given by a beautiful woman."

"Thank you," Faith said, resisting the urge to squirm in discomfort as she loaded the books into the case and closed the door. "Book preservation is my passion."

"I do appreciate fine books, though my interest is mostly in the hunt for the perfect addition to my personal library. As Dickens said, 'There is a passion for hunting something deeply implanted in the human breast.' I like the thrill of pursuit." He grinned at her, showing off large white teeth behind his mustache and beard.

"I am afraid the hunting gene must have passed me by," Faith said as she tried to ease around Charles to return to the other guests.

He shifted position to stay directly in front of her. "You sound like a woman of moderation. I admire that, however much I cannot say I practice it. As Dickens said, 'Subdue your appetites, my dears, and you've conquered human nature.'"

"You certainly know your Dickens," Faith said, again trying to get around him. "Please do excuse me. I don't want to neglect the others. Someone may have questions about book preservation."

"If I must share, then I must." Charles reluctantly gave way, moving to one side to reveal Octavia behind him. The older woman glared into Faith's eyes with absolute fury. Faith was so alarmed by the woman's ferocity that she froze. What could she have done to upset Octavia so deeply?

"Charles!" Everyone turned to see Evelyn sweeping toward them. Even without Victorian finery, there was a sense of weight and importance to the woman as she drew the attention of everyone around her. "You must stop hogging Miss Newberry. I have questions."

Charles's lips pressed together in a tight line, but he gave a sharp nod. Octavia took the opportunity to rush to his side and take his arm. He turned his attention unhappily toward the older woman, his smile anything but genuine.

Evelyn linked her arm through Faith's and towed her away, murmuring, "You were like a deer caught in the headlights. Tell me, was it Charles's boorish attention or Octavia's death stare?"

"I suppose I do get a little overwhelmed sometimes, especially right after a presentation," Faith said, not wanting to gossip about guests. "I'm so very sorry about what happened to you last night. Have the police said anything about leads?"

"No." Evelyn waved a hand. "It's not of great consequence. As I said before, I'm heavily insured, and I was just spouting off about holding Castleton Manor responsible. I'm annoyed, don't get me wrong about it, but I mostly hated how frightened my darling kitties were. Which leads me to what I wanted to ask you. Is that little cutie yours?" She pointed toward Watson, who sat before the fireplace delicately washing his face.

"Yes, that's Watson. I'm so happy to work in an environment that welcomes pets."

"That is one of my favorite things about this resort," Evelyn said agreeably. "I have two tailless cats of my own, though Watson doesn't look exactly like a Manx. What breed is he?"

"I truly don't know. A mix of things, I imagine, but Watson wasn't born with a bobbed tail. He had some sort of accident when he was a kitten. He was in rough shape when I found him."

"You must be his hero," Evelyn said.

Faith laughed. "I'm not sure Watson sees it quite that way, but he's certainly been my hero once or twice."

"Sounds mysterious. I hope you'll tell me all about it. In fact, I would love for Watson to meet my kitties. They're terrified of dogs, so I can't take them around with me, but I'm absolutely certain they would love to make a new friend. Would you consider bringing Watson and having lunch with us in my suite? And while you're there, I have a book I'd like to show you and ask your opinion on."

Faith hesitated, wondering how Marlene would feel about her lunching with a guest. But after all, Evelyn wanted to ask her about a book, and that *was* her job. "That sounds wonderful. You're in the Jane Austen Suite, right?"

"Exactly. It's so lavish I'm half-afraid to sit on anything, though the kitties love it. I'm flexible about time since I'm officially on vacation. When do you normally take your lunch break?" Faith told her and Evelyn clapped her hands together softly. "Excellent. Since we have a date, I'll release you to your admirers." She turned sharply and strode toward the library door.

Such a dramatic person, Faith thought as she turned back toward the milling group and began answering questions about climate control and the challenges of old paper and ink. Fortunately Charles showed no further interest in chatting with her. Instead he seemed to be trying to talk to Caroline around her mother. Since Caroline was equally trying to stay away from him, it made for an interesting chase around the library that Faith caught from the corner of her eye.

Several of the guests had extensive book collections, and they kept Faith busy with their many questions until lunch was announced. The library emptied out, and Faith tidied up a bit, then closed the library to head upstairs with Watson trotting along beside her. "I do hope you'll behave," she told him. "Don't be mean to Evelyn's cats."

Watson flicked his stub of a tail.

When they reached the suite, Faith scooped up the cat before knocking on the door. Watson could be a little unpredictable, and she wanted to be certain he didn't do anything to upset Evelyn, since she'd had enough difficulty the night before.

The door flew open just as Faith knocked. Evelyn had changed clothes into something fluttery that made her seem as if she'd stepped from an old black-and-white movie.

"I hope I'm not late," Faith said.

"No, your timing is wonderful." She waved Faith in. The suites were the only part of the manor not decorated for Christmas, except for the arches of greenery over the outer doorframes.

Not that the Jane Austen Suite needed any further decor. Done in an impressive French Regency confection of pale pink and gold, the raised bed area and the sitting room were draped in sumptuous fabrics and lavish details.

Faith had been in this suite before but not under such pleasant circumstances. She didn't have much time to dwell on the past, though, as Evelyn's two cats greeted them the moment they came in, meowing with excitement. Both had the long back legs that were indicative of Manx cats and gave them a rabbit-like gait. Beyond that, the cats were strikingly different. One was marmalade orange with a white chin and round head. The other was a dainty calico.

Faith put Watson down on the floor, and the two Manx cats immediately rushed over and began rubbing their heads on him and purring loudly.

"The marmalade cat is Dora and the other is Little Nell. Good Dickens names, both of them. I knew my girls would like such a handsome fellow," Evelyn said. "Now come and see my book."

Faith followed her to the delicate Regency desk and watched her pick up a book bound in worn brown fabric. Evelyn handled the book casually while Faith watched in alarm, especially when Evelyn thrust it at her.

"I didn't bring my gloves," Faith protested.

"Don't worry about that. This is a reproduction. It only looks old. I do have an antique copy, which is extremely rare, but I leave it at home, where it has the proper conditions. This is what I call my travel version. Are you familiar with the book?"

Faith admired the book in her hands and opened to the flyleaf. It was a copy of *What Shall We Have for Dinner?* by Lady Maria

Clutterbuck. Faith smiled. "I know this book. Lady Clutterbuck was a nom de plume for Charles Dickens's wife. I believe the authentic first editions were actually paperbound, though it's impossible to know for sure, as none of those first editions have survived to the present day."

"How tragic that must be for the literary world," Evelyn said. "I know how valuable old first editions are. Anyway, I thought it would be fun to bring my copy along and see how the food here lines up with Lady Clutterbuck's preferences. I find the cookbook rather meat-heavy. Apparently Dickens was fond of hearty meals."

Faith leafed through the book of menus and saw that one of them was built around roast goose. "I believe the manor is planning to have goose for dinner one night."

"Terrific," Evelyn said. She gestured toward two chairs. "Come and sit. You'd think these chairs were torturous with their straight backs, but they're actually surprisingly comfortable."

Faith took a seat and they settled into a light conversation about books. She was so wrapped up in the engaging conversation that she didn't notice Watson's reaction to Dora and Nell's affection.

The cat shook off the purring puffs of perfumed fluff and darted under his human's chair, hoping the two silly cats would take the hint. To his extreme displeasure, they seemed incapable of grasping any subtlety. The way they were acting, he would have thought they were dogs.

When both female cats squeezed under the chair around him, he rushed out toward the heavy curtains nearby. If he was lucky, the perplexing creatures would be claustrophobic and leave him alone.

His plan seemed to work, and he peered dolefully out at his human. He could tell by her cheerful baring of teeth and her relaxed body language that they were likely to be in the suite for a long time. If he'd been offered a treat, it might have been bearable, but as it was, he had no intention of spending the afternoon with his fur being ruffled and his nose being nuzzled. It was undignified.

The cat shifted his weight and something moved under his back foot. It startled him so much that he jumped. He peered around, hoping the humans had not witnessed his humiliating overreaction. Though neither human had noticed, his fright had rustled the curtain, and he could see the two felines heading his way. Annoyed, he peered at his foot to see what had created the problem. It was an odd piece of slick paper.

He snatched it up in his mouth, intending to return to his human's chair and chew the bit of paper into tatters for frightening him into giving away his hiding spot. He dashed out of his hiding place and leaped onto his human's lap, hoping for a little time to himself during which to destroy the offending paper.

When Watson jumped onto her lap, Faith immediately saw something clenched in his mouth. In alarm, she pulled it away before he could chew it up and swallow it. "I'm sorry," Faith said, mildly embarrassed. "Watson seems to have found your playing cards. He's torn this one up a bit."

Evelyn barely glanced at the card in Faith's hand. "That's not mine. I didn't bring any playing cards. It must have been left from the last guest."

"How odd," Faith said as she turned the card over in her hand. "The maids are usually extremely thorough here. It isn't like them to miss something." The playing card, a queen of hearts, was unusual. It featured a beautifully drawn figure in a long Victorian gown. As Faith held the card closer to her eyes, she saw it was so detailed that it resembled a portrait more than a playing card—and something about the idealized face was familiar.

"Everyone makes mistakes," Evelyn said mildly, drawing her away from her study of the card. "Though I certainly hope a little poor housekeeping and a burglary are the extent of the problems this week."

Before Faith could reply, a firm knock on the door brought Evelyn to her feet. "That must be lunch."

Faith watched Evelyn hurry across the room, then glanced back down at the card. The maids at the manor were excellent. Faith knew how spotless they kept the library. Books were notorious dust collectors, so if the staff could keep them clean, they surely would not miss a playing card on the floor. Unless the card hadn't been there when the maids cleaned. Could she be holding a clue dropped by the burglar?

5

Though the lunch was delicious and Faith enjoyed her chat with Evelyn, the visit ended rather abruptly when Watson raced across the room and climbed Faith like a tree. He didn't stop until he was perched on her shoulder, glaring balefully down at the other cats. He even hissed at them for good measure.

"I should probably go," Faith said as she tried to pry Watson free of her sweater without leaving holes from his claws. "When Watson gets in a mood, there's no telling what he might do."

"I can sympathize," Evelyn said. "Sometimes Dora and Nell rush around like lions are chasing them. Plus, neither of them gets along well with dogs. Poor Dora is so totally dog-phobic that I would have to sedate the poor darlings to take them downstairs with me. Dora gets crazy if she even smells dog on my clothes." She sighed. "I could tell they loved visiting with Watson, and I know I enjoyed our chat. Thanks for popping up for a visit."

"I had a lovely time."

When Faith was out in the hall with Watson in her arms, she examined the playing card again and wondered if she should show it to the police. It was a unique card, and Faith couldn't shake the feeling that it was connected to the burglary somehow. On the other hand, the police had already searched the room, and it *was* just a playing card. Officer Laddy wasn't above lecturing her about leaving the investigation to the police. She slipped the card into the pocket of her slacks. *I'll hold on to it and decide later.* Even if it was a clue, it was hardly a hot one since any prints that might have been on the shiny surface would have been smeared by Watson's mouth and Faith's handling.

Watson squirmed in her arms as she started down the stairs. "Forget it," she said softly. "I'll put you down when we're back in the library. I don't need you running all over and getting into things."

The cat gave her such an annoyed glare that it was almost as if he could understand and take offense at her remark.

She was so caught up in her interaction with Watson that at first she didn't notice the sound of an argument going on near the base of the cantilevered marble stairs. Faith stopped, wondering if she should go back upstairs and head down in the elevator or one of the other smaller flights of stairs to avoid disturbing whoever was engaged in the heated exchange.

As she pondered her next move, one voice rose particularly loud, and Faith definitely recognized it.

"Don't spoil this for me or I'll never forgive you!" Octavia Skimsby screeched. "Charles is always nice to you, so stop being so unpleasant to him."

"Nice?" Caroline said. "You consider his behavior toward me nice?"

"Oh, Caroline, you clearly don't know what men are like."

Faith drifted down another step to hear the quieter reply. "I know how a good man acts," Caroline said. "Mother, Charles isn't interested in you. He's a cad and does that smarmy flirting with every woman here."

"Not true," Octavia snapped. "He doesn't show Evelyn the kind of attention that he shows me."

"Because Evelyn won't put up with it," Caroline said. "And neither should you. And neither should I. It's not cute or charming, and I don't want it directed at me."

"You don't know what you're talking about, you foolish girl. Naturally, Charles is friendly to everyone he meets, but it's not the same. And since Charles is going to be your stepfather, I would think you'd want to build a better relationship with him."

"He's not nice. He's repulsive," Caroline said. "Didn't you see him flirting with the librarian? She certainly didn't appear to like the attention, so I doubt she'd typify it as friendly."

"So now you're using the behavior of hired help as proof of your position. How very sad. I will expect your apology by dinnertime."

Faith heard the sound of heels on the gallery floor. Clearly Octavia had flounced off, but was Caroline still down there? Faith didn't want to show up now. It would look like she'd been listening, which she had, of course. Watson squirmed again, obviously annoyed by Faith's tightening grip on him as she worked out what to do.

"Whoever is on the stairs, you can come down," Caroline called out. "My mother and I are done acting silly."

Faith's heart skipped a beat. *Caught.* With no way to avoid it, she walked down the rest of the stairs, her cheeks flaming. "I'm so sorry. I didn't mean to eavesdrop. I wasn't sure whether to go back up or interrupt . . ."

"Don't worry about it," Caroline said. "If Mother and I wanted privacy, we shouldn't have been arguing in public." She reached out and chucked Watson under the chin. "Who is this handsome feline?"

"This is Watson. He was at my presentation this morning, curled up in front of the fire."

"Oh, now I remember. I thought he was the library cat."

"I suppose he is now," Faith said. "But Watson belongs to me. Or rather, I belong to him. We've been together since he was a kitten." As Caroline scratched Watson's head, her face relaxed at the cat's rumbling purr. "You've made a friend for life now. Watson loves for anyone to fuss over him. He's such a ham."

Caroline scratched the cat under the chin and was rewarded with an even louder purr. "He's lovely. I wish I could have a pet. Mother is allergic, and she lives with me."

"I hope she's not having too much trouble with her allergies. We do allow pets here, so she's likely to come into contact with them all over the manor."

Caroline waved away the concern. "Actually I'm pretty sure Mother is only allergic to the *idea* of my having a pet. She doesn't like to share attention." She rubbed Watson's ears, then pulled her hand away and hugged herself. "I don't know why I argue with my mother. There's never any point. Life is easier if I just go along."

"That doesn't sound like a very happy way to live," Faith said.

"Neither is being in conflict all the time."

"And there's no conflict if you pretend to agree with her?"

Again Caroline sighed. "No. If I agree with her, then the criticism is about my clothes or my hair or my posture. You're right. It isn't exactly a great way to live, but I keep telling myself it's only temporary."

"Because your mother is going to marry Charles and move out?"

Caroline laughed drily. "Charles isn't going to marry my mother. She doesn't have the looks or the youth that a man like him pursues. I honestly don't know why he gives her as much attention as he does. He acts like most of the other women in the society are invisible. Unless he thinks they're attractive."

"You don't seem to have a very high opinion of the man."

"I think he's a player. I'm just waiting for him to lose interest and move on to one of the wealthier women in the society. We certainly don't have the money to interest a man like him, though I suspect Mother has led him to believe we have considerably more than we do. She certainly taxes our budget buying the tiresome man presents."

Faith felt uncomfortable with so much intimate knowledge of the guests' personal lives. On impulse, she pulled the playing card from her pocket. "Excuse me for changing the subject, but have you ever seen a playing card like this one?"

Caroline took the card from her and peered closely at the portrait of the queen, and then she laughed, this time with real humor. "I definitely recognize this card. I posed for it." She held the card up beside her face. "Recognize me?"

Faith leaned closer, but the overly idealized portrait bore little resemblance to the woman before her. Still, this accounted for her flash of recognition when Watson brought her the card. She wasn't sure what to say.

"Don't worry. I don't think it looks like me either. I sat for the portrait because my mother insisted. It was some favor for Charles. Beyond that, I don't really know much about it. Do you have the rest of the deck? I never did get to see the whole thing."

"No, I only have the one card. So this deck of cards might belong to Charles?"

Caroline shrugged. "I suppose, but he was having them professionally printed by his publishing company. They're for sale on the society's website. So anyone could have bought a deck."

Faith ran a finger over the face of the card. *Interesting.*

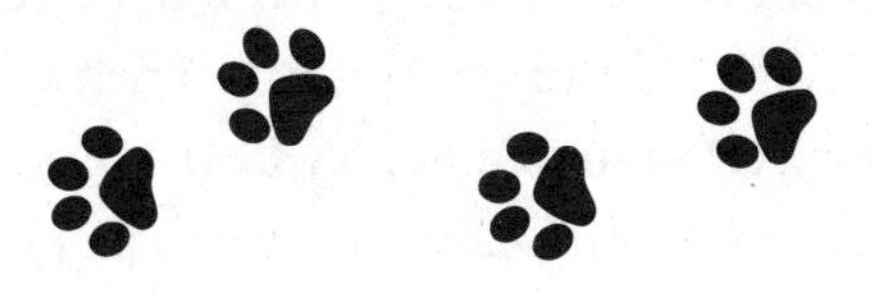

The rest of the afternoon was uneventful, though Faith had visits from several guests with more questions related to her presentation. She was delighted that the information proved so interesting to the society members, but she was glad when darkness fell outside the library and she was able to lock up and head for the cottage for dinner with Watson. Though she was due back to the manor for the second *Christmas Carol* reading later in the evening, she planned to take full advantage of her brief respite.

As always, the front door of the old gardener's cottage that had become Faith's home glowed with golden light that made it seem warmer on the dark night. When she walked in with Watson on her heels, she quickly got a fire going in the fireplace before starting dinner. Her grandmother's cuddly old quilt lay in the chair near the fireplace as if inviting her to take a seat. *As soon as I'm done eating, you and I are spending a few minutes of quality time together.*

She and Watson had barely finished their dinner when Faith was startled by a knock at the door. She opened it to see Brooke, a fretful expression on her face. "I'm sorry to drop in unannounced," she said, "but I'm so steamed that I just had to see a friendly face before I went home."

"No problem. I understand those days." Faith gestured for Brooke to come in. "I have some chowder on the stove. Would you like a mug of it? Watson and I just ate."

"A cup of chowder sounds heavenly. It's been a difficult day." Brooke stomped the snow from her boots and pulled off her knit cap, leaving her short hair floating with static electricity.

Grinning, Faith led the way to the kitchen and reached into the cupboard for a clean soup mug. "Catastrophes in the kitchen?"

"No, the guests seem to love the Victorian menus," Brooke said, her tone lighter. "Since I helped with the menu planning, the head chef keeps turning the accolades back to me, which is very generous."

Faith ladled seafood chowder into the mug and handed it to Brooke with a spoon. "Then what made the day rough?"

Brooke blew across the top of the soup, then glared into the mug. "Charles. He complained about me after all. Marlene read me the riot act about it this afternoon."

"I'm so sorry to hear that," Faith said. "Do you want to sit in front of the fire to eat? It's very soothing. I'll even let you borrow my grandmother's quilt."

"I can use all the soothing I can get," Brooke said as she followed Faith out to the cozy chairs facing the fire. As soon as she sat, Watson jumped onto Brooke's lap. She scratched behind one of his ears. "Is this love, or do you just smell fish soup and hope I'll give you some?"

"Probably a little of both," Faith said. "Though Watson already had dinner, so he has no reason to beg."

As Watson settled innocently into her lap, Brooke sipped a spoonful of the chowder. "This is fantastic."

"Probably because it's the recipe you gave me." She watched as Brooke took several more spoonfuls. "I'm sorry you had such an awful day."

"Would you believe Marlene actually threatened to fire me?"

"Fire you?" Faith had been afraid something like that would happen.

"Well, indirectly. She said, 'You are a fine sous-chef, Miss Milner, but you are not irreplaceable.' You'd think I mugged the man instead of simply offering his company the opportunity to publish a good cookbook."

"I truly thought Charles was going to let it go."

"He's disgusting. Acting all creepy and flirty to my face and then complaining about me behind my back." Brooke sighed and took another sip. "This is *really* good. I think you make it better than I do."

"It's the fire. Everything tastes better in front of a fire."

Brooke leaned back in the chair. "That's probably it. I should make this for myself at home, but I tend to avoid making seafood in front of Diva and Bling. It always makes them nervous." Diva and Bling were Brooke's pet angelfish, who seemed to have a surprisingly deep emotional life, at least in Brooke's imagination.

"I don't have that problem with Watson. I made a huge batch and froze it in smaller servings so I could have some whenever I wanted. I hope you don't mind, but I shared the recipe with Aunt Eileen, and it's her favorite now too." Eileen Piper was Faith's aunt and the head librarian in town. She hosted the Candle House Book Club that included Faith and Brooke.

"Of course I don't mind. You know how much I love Eileen." Brooke lowered the empty mug to her lap and Watson stuck his face in it.

"I'm totally on your side in the Charles situation," Faith said. "But I might mildly object to the way you're corrupting my cat."

"There is such a thing as being too good," Brooke said. "I'm saving Watson from that possibility."

"Right." Faith stood and took the mug, earning herself a dirty look from the cat in the process, which was impossible to take seriously because of a bit of chowder on his nose. "I want to show you something that might be related to the robbery last night."

Brooke's eyes widened and she leaned forward. "Oh, are you sleuthing? You know how much I love a good mystery. Tell me it points to Charles or Marlene as the culprit and you'll really cheer me up."

"I think it might be hard for Charles to burglarize rooms while he's doing a public reading from Dickens," Faith said drily.

"A girl can dream. Okay, fill me in on your investigation."

"This is a police matter, and I'm not getting involved," Faith insisted as she slipped her hand into her pocket and handed over the card. "But Watson found this up in Evelyn Pugh's suite today."

While Brooke examined it, Faith carried her friend's mug to the kitchen and put it in the sink. When she walked back out, Brooke said, "This is pretty. It's certainly an unusual playing card. The picture almost seems like a real portrait. Did you ask Mrs. Pugh about it?"

"Yes. She said she'd never seen it. But Caroline Skimsby told me she is the person who posed for it, though it doesn't resemble her very well. These cards were commissioned for the society by Charles."

"See? It does point toward him. I'm telling you, he robbed Mrs. Pugh," Brooke said. "I'd love to see him arrested."

"You still have to overcome the fact that he was giving a performance in front of the whole society at the time." Faith settled back in her chair. "And in front of you and me too."

"You are entirely too determined to rain on my parade," Brooke said. "I would say that card definitely ties the burglary to the Dickens Society."

"Maybe. I don't know. Caroline told me the cards are for sale on the society's website. Technically, someone at the manor could have bought a deck."

"Sounds like a stretch. I think you should hand this over to Bryan Laddy. In fact, I think you should call Officer Laddy right now and ask him over. You can give him the card and I'll stand behind you and wave in a cute way."

"Aren't you public-spirited tonight?" Faith said.

"Come on. Seeing a good-looking man in uniform would definitely brighten my miserable day."

"As much as I want to brighten your day, I'm not sure this playing card would impress the police much. It's been chewed on by a cat and handled by several people. And it's definitely not something he'd appreciate being called out for on a cold night."

"Spoilsport," Brooke grumped, though she sounded decidedly cheerier than she had when she arrived.

"It's about to get worse," Faith warned. "I have to go back to the manor for the second *Christmas Carol* reading. You're welcome to come with me or stay and keep Watson company, but I have to go."

Brooke shuddered. "I definitely don't want to go with you. One of the chef's assistants is handling the refreshments tonight, and I do not want to run into Charles. I might kick him in the shins. I believe I'll go home and have a nice hot soak in the tub and tell my woes to Diva and Bling. Though I probably shouldn't. They get so upset when I have a hard day."

Faith was always amused by how Brooke projected her own emotions onto her two angelfish, while they simply radiated the same calm fish always did. "You should watch Diva and Bling swim for a while. Studies show that it's very relaxing."

"Maybe I will," Brooke said. "And while I'm watching fish swim, I'll think about how I could be chatting with a certain handsome police officer if my best friend had only been willing to call him."

"Someday I hope you find it in your heart to forgive me," Faith said as she showed Brooke out. Then she quickly stowed the leftover soup in the fridge and put out the fire before slipping into her coat for the walk back to the manor.

Watson meowed at her.

"No, you cannot come. And don't go sneaking out. Remember how cold you got last night? You just stay home and wait for me."

For once, Watson settled down obediently on top of the quilt in the chair and curled up for a nap. Faith wasn't sure if that was good or not. Her cat could be quite an actor when he set his mind to it. For good measure, she pointed a finger at him and said, "Stay!"

He opened one eye and gave her an expression that clearly said, "Really?"

The cold outside seemed to have sharpened since Faith had made the walk home for dinner, so she kept up a brisk pace when heading back, slowing only enough to avoid slipping on any icy spots on the path. As a result, she was slightly breathless when she arrived at the manor.

She felt the warm embrace of the excellent heating system as she entered. She would have sighed with pleasure, but then she spotted someone who definitely cooled her enthusiasm—Marlene.

The assistant manager barreled across the main hall. "The reading has been canceled," she said. "You'll need to go to the library and be certain everyone knows."

"Why is the event canceled?" Faith asked.

Marlene's sour expression tightened even more and she dropped the shrill tone of her voice. "There's been another burglary. Another guest was robbed."

"Are the police on their way?" Faith asked, chilled all over again at the thought of another burglary.

"They're upstairs now." Marlene's tone conveyed just how much she hated the idea of the police in the manor.

"Earlier today Watson found a possible clue in Evelyn Pugh's room. I'd like to go up and give it to the officers since they're here."

Marlene's gaze sharpened. "What were you doing in Mrs. Pugh's room? You're not poking around in these burglaries, are you? As much as I'd like this all to be settled, you are a librarian, not a police officer. Stick to your job."

Faith silently counted to ten to calm her annoyance at Marlene's tone. "I wasn't investigating. I was lunching. Mrs. Pugh invited me up for lunch. She wanted her cats to socialize with Watson, and she wanted to show me a book."

Marlene sniffed. "I suppose that's reasonable. I cannot imagine why people are so daffy over pets. I'll walk up with you, as I really should be monitoring the police while they are upstairs. But you'll need to go straight to the library afterward."

"Of course."

As they walked up the stairs, Marlene continued to talk about the burglaries. "This time the burglar broke into the Daphne du Maurier Suite, which is one of our small suites. Why would someone rob that room when we have much fancier rooms on the same floor? I could understand picking the Jane Austen Suite. Obviously whoever stays there is quite well off, but then the next logical choice is the Agatha Christie Suite, where Octavia and Caroline Skimsby are staying."

"Apparently the burglar is choosing based on something other than the size of the rooms," Faith said as they topped the stairs and turned into the hall.

On the second floor, the Christmas decorations were more understated, although, like the Austen Suite, each door had an evergreen swag laced with gold ribbon. Unlike the nondescript halls of most hotels and resorts, Castleton Manor had beautiful hand-carved walnut moldings and dark wood flooring, continuing the style of the downstairs.

Officer Laddy stood in the hall with Wolfe Jaxon. Both men nodded at Faith, Wolfe offering a warm smile.

"It would certainly appear that you're right, Faith," Wolfe told her. "The thief must have inside information about the belongings of at least some of the society members."

"That looks like the case, from what I can tell." Officer Laddy glanced past Faith to Marlene. "As much as I appreciate Miss Newberry's insights, it might be better if you didn't lead staff tours up here right now. I have not completed my examination of the crime scene."

"I would hardly do that," Marlene said, affront dripping from her words. "I wouldn't even have *you* up here if I could avoid it."

Faith decided to intervene. "Actually I need to give you something." She handed over the card and explained how Watson had found it in Evelyn's suite.

Wolfe chuckled. "It sounds like it might be time to put Watson on the police force."

Faith laughed lightly at the joke, but Officer Laddy was clearly not amused by the suggestion that a cat could assist in his job. He pulled an evidence bag from his pocket and held it open for Faith to insert the card. Then he took out a second bag, this one already containing a card that was nearly identical to the one Faith had handed over. "We found this inside on the table where the stolen items should have been. Since we now know there was one at the first crime as well, it appears this thief has a calling card."

"Literally." Leaning forward to get a better look, Faith wondered if this card represented someone from the society as well. The queen was very detailed but clearly not Caroline, though the coal-black hair and pointed chin did feel faintly familiar. "When I spoke to Caroline Skimsby earlier today, she told me that Charles commissioned the art for these playing cards. They're for sale on the society's website, but Mr. Huffam may have some way of knowing who in the society has bought them. Caroline said she does not own a deck, even though that first card is her portrait. Or it's supposed to be."

The officer frowned at the card Faith had given him. "Do you know where your cat found this card? Was it left at the location of Mrs. Pugh's jewelry?"

"I don't know. I didn't see Watson pick it up. I suspect he got it from the floor. But Evelyn has two cats of her own, so even if the thief left the card out in the open, the cats may have relocated it before she returned to her room, just as Watson did."

"That's true. I'll contact Mr. Huffam and see if he has a list of people who own the cards." Officer Laddy's lips turned up in a wry smile. "Since that would make the case considerably easier, it's probably safe to assume he does not have such a list."

"That sounds pessimistic," Wolfe said.

"I find I feel increasingly pessimistic every time we're called out here to Castleton Manor. When this place has a crime, it's always complicated."

"We certainly don't do anything to encourage crime," Marlene huffed. "Complicated or otherwise."

"Did the burglar steal jewelry again?" Faith asked.

"The owner of the room had a vintage cuff link collection," the officer said. "It wasn't as valuable as Mrs. Pugh's Victorian jewelry, but it was still impressive."

"I never thought of cuff links as being comparable in value to necklaces and such," Faith said. "We had a past guest with a lovely collection of Sherlock Holmes-inspired cuff links, but I don't think they were particularly rare or valuable."

Wolfe spoke up: "You'd be surprised by how pricey cuff links can be. I have a pair of vintage mother-of-pearl cuff links worth well over $1,000, and they are far from the most expensive ones I've seen."

"Apparently Mrs. Pugh's collection was quite well-known in the society," Officer Laddy said. "I'll be interested to know if the same can be said for Mr. Alried's cuff links."

"Alried?" Faith echoed.

"Morton Alried," Wolfe replied. He clapped Officer Laddy on the back. "Thanks for your good work on this. I certainly would like to find the thief before we have any more incidents. Our guests need to feel safe here."

"I'll do my best," the officer said. "It's my job."

"Please excuse me, gentlemen," Faith said. "Marlene told me to go to the library in case anyone comes for the reading. As soon as I'm sure everyone is informed, I'll be going home."

"That will be fine," Officer Laddy said. "Thank you for turning in the card."

"I'll see you tomorrow," Wolfe said to Faith. "I'm looking forward to the tree lighting."

"Me too."

When Faith reached the gallery downstairs, she found Charles standing near the little grouping of slender Christmas trees under the statue of Agatha Christie, ranting to a small circle of society members. Once again, the group was decked out in full Victorian dress.

Charles caught sight of Faith and pointed at her. "How dare you people cancel a Dickens Society function without consulting me!"

Heads bobbed all around him as the society members sided with their leader.

"Do you know how long it takes to put this on?" an older woman demanded, lifting a handful of her full skirt.

"I wasn't part of the decision to cancel the event," Faith said. "However, I'm sure it was made to facilitate the solving of a serious crime, Mr. Huffam."

"Yes, yes, I heard about poor old Alried's cuff links." He waved a hand dismissively. "I can't imagine why anyone would bother with a whole collection of the fussy things. I find two pairs takes care of all the events I need."

"Is Morton unharmed?" The question came from a tall, thin man who put Faith in mind of a well-dressed scarecrow.

"I believe he is," Faith assured him, assuming she would have been informed if he were not. "I don't really know any details. I was asked to come and tell you that we'd be canceling tonight's reading, but I see that Mr. Huffam has already handled that."

"Perhaps we can do it tomorrow afternoon," a hawkish woman of about Faith's age said, nervously smoothing her own heavy velvet skirts. "It's the only time that will fit the schedule."

"How tiresome," Charles said. "I was hoping to use that time to catch up on some business phone calls. But I can't let the society down."

"Well," the older woman chimed in, "if the reading is truly called off for the evening, then I'm going up to my room to count my jewelry."

"Oh?" the scarecrow said. "Do you have a lot of jewelry, Emily?"

The woman laughed, a thin cackle. "No, so it'll be a quick count."

The small group of society members headed for the stairs, all except for Charles. He approached Faith with a broad smile. "Ah, alone at last. I would love to chat with you about Dickens."

"Since the reading is canceled, I'll be heading home." Faith crossed her arms over her chest.

"Don't rush off." Charles stepped closer, well within her personal space. "You could come up to my room. I have some very fine cognac that I would love to share with you. It's so boorish to drink alone."

Not in this lifetime, Faith thought, repressing a shudder at the thought of being alone with him. "That's generous of you, but it's getting late and I have to work tomorrow."

"But you would have been here far later than this if the reading had gone as planned, so this is all time you intended to give to us anyway. I'm sure you wouldn't want to leave a guest lonely and unhappy." The threat in his voice was obvious.

Faith began to think she wouldn't be able to get by Charles. She was sure Wolfe would back her up if Charles reported her, but she couldn't say the same of Marlene. Though Marlene would certainly not sanction Faith going to Charles's room under any circumstances, she also hated when guests complained. Plus, the assistant manager seemed to find every opportunity to give Faith and every other employee a hard time.

"It wouldn't be appropriate for me to have a drink with you," she said. "You're a guest and I work here. The staff is under rather strict rules about our behavior." She hoped her reference to the staff would remind him of his disdain for anyone under his perceived social rank and get him to leave her alone.

Instead, he winked slyly. “I won’t tell anyone. I like a little vice. As Dickens said, ‘Vices are sometimes only virtues carried to excess!’”

Faith started to feel real alarm at the man’s obnoxious persistence. Then she caught sight of someone in a dark red dress hurrying down the gallery toward them as fast as yards of taffeta would allow.

As soon as she recognized the person, Faith spotted an opportunity to put an end to Charles’s attention. “I’m sure you can find someone who would enjoy sharing your cognac,” Faith said, her voice loud enough to carry in the huge gallery. “I heard you are quite seriously involved with Octavia Skimsby.” She raised her hand to gesture toward Octavia, who was now behind Charles.

But before she could speak, Charles burst out laughing. “You think I would be interested in that made-up old crone? Hardly. Though her daughter is certainly a lovely little thing. Her, I wouldn’t mind getting to know better.”

At his remark, Octavia shrieked, causing Charles to spin around to face her. The older woman flew at him, her face distorted with rage. She clawed at his face with her long, carefully manicured nails. She managed to rake a row of scratches down the side of his face before he caught her arms and shoved her to the floor.

“You keep your hands off me,” he snarled. He touched the side of his face and then looked at his bloody fingertips. “You’ll be sorry you did that.”

Octavia sat on the floor, panting. She sneered at Charles. “I won’t be the one who is sorry. ‘There are strings in the human heart that had better not be vibrated.’ You had best remember your Dickens and the bad ends a villain can come to.”

Charles didn't reply to that—he merely swept around her and off down the gallery hall without another word.

Faith was horrified. As much as she appreciated being rid of Charles for now, she was stunned by the violence. She reached a tentative hand out to Octavia, who slapped it away.

"I don't need your help." The older woman got awkwardly to her feet, an almost comical procedure due to the full skirts of her dress. Once she was standing she gave Faith an unfriendly once-over. "I know your social-climbing type. You stay away from Charles, do you hear me, missy?"

"I assure you—"

"I don't need your assurances," Octavia said. "But I'll give you one of mine. If I see you flirting with that man again, you'll be deeply and permanently sorry."

Stunned that anyone would think she had been flirting with Charles, Faith stood speechless as Octavia followed Charles down the gallery hall, her taffeta skirts rustling.

7

After a frightening dream of Octavia perched on her chest, poking her nose with a bony finger and threatening her, Faith woke to Watson sitting in the same spot, peering intently into her face. Faith pushed him gently off onto the comforter. "You won't get breakfast any faster by giving me nightmares," she said as she swung her legs over the side of the bed.

She wasn't scheduled to open the library until this afternoon as the society program was packed with activities that would make it unlikely anyone would want to check out the library's collection before then. One of those activities was a vendor day in the gallery, and Faith was eager to see what Dickens-themed merchandise might be available. Although her Christmas shopping was mostly done, she still had a few small gifts to buy, and the vendor fairs often provided access to unusual items Faith wouldn't find in the Lighthouse Bay shops.

After a hot breakfast for herself and Watson, Faith shut the cottage door very firmly in his face. "Stay home and out of trouble," she warned, though she knew it was probably pointless. Watson was an escape artist who put Houdini to shame and often got himself into the most unlikely—and sometimes dangerous—spots.

The crisp morning was unusually bright, with none of the gray skies that might have dulled the Christmas cheer. As she walked along with her hands deep in her coat pockets, Faith appreciated the little touches along the path. Even though few guests would be likely to wander through the gardens, there were still tiny lights hung on the trees near the main house and evergreen branches and wreaths nearly everywhere. Greenery spiraled up the old-fashioned lampposts that lined the paths, and wreaths hung in the windows of the manor house.

Faith stomped the bits of snow and ice from her boots and walked through the vestibule and main hall. Slender Christmas trees in tall urns twinkled with white lights and gold garlands and balls. When she turned into the two-story gallery, more greenery, lights, and gilt ornaments continued the Christmas decor, though some of the larger displays had been moved to make room for over a dozen different vendors. To fit the Victorian theme, the vendors wore period outfits, and each had a wheeled cart from which to display his or her Victorian- and/or Christmas-themed items.

Faith picked up a clever jumping jack for her nephew and a tiny hand-turned wooden top. She had the jumping jack wrapped, but she slipped the top into the pocket of her jacket, thinking she'd give it to Oliver as soon as she saw him. Although her sister scolded her for spoiling him, Faith always brought a small toy or treat on every visit, which Oliver would try to guess. Whenever her sister commented on the gifts, Faith always told her that aunts were supposed to act like that.

Moving along to a distressed-wood cart with a tattered canopy, Faith was immediately enchanted by the wide selection of Christmas ornaments, all with either a Victorian or steampunk design. She squealed aloud when she spotted the perfect Christmas gift for her friend Midge. Faith had become close friends with all the members of the Candle House Book Club after they welcomed her so warmly. When the club had drawn names for Christmas gifts, Faith got Midge. With her quirky sense of style, Midge had proved harder to buy for than Faith anticipated. She'd scoured all of Lighthouse Bay for the perfect gift, and now she held it in her hand.

"I see you've found our little dog ornaments," the vendor told Faith. "Those are my favorites. It's so funny to think of dogs dressed up."

Faith nearly laughed aloud at that since Midge regularly dressed up her beloved Chihuahua, Atticus. Faith personally thought Atticus must be the world's most patient dog. Watson wouldn't tolerate one of the adorable little outfits for any length of time. She'd tried to get him into a sweater once, thinking he might be cold, but he would have none of it, and she had never made another attempt.

"I have a friend whose dog looks exactly like this," Faith said as she turned the tiny porcelain Chihuahua ornament around in her hand to admire the top hat, scarf, and riding goggles. "Costume and all."

"Your friend must be an interesting person."

"She is," Faith agreed. "And so is her dog. I'll take this. Do you have a box?"

"Give me just a second." The vendor bent to root through bags on a shelf at the back of the pushcart.

Faith glanced idly over the rest of the items, then started. There were packs of playing cards in a pile on one corner. The design on the cover was exactly like the card Watson had found. Faith picked up a box, wondering how one of these cards had ended up on the floor of a burgled suite. "These are very unusual cards."

The vendor straightened. "Those cards were commissioned by the president of the Charles Dickens Society. Several of the vendors have them. The face cards all represent specific members of the society." The woman peered more closely at Faith. "Are you a member? I don't remember seeing you on any of the cards, but the portraits may be a little stylized. I don't recognize most of the people portrayed on them. No eye for it, I guess."

"I'm not a member. I'm the librarian here at the manor. But these are lovely. I would like a deck, please."

"It'd be my pleasure."

"You don't happen to know who the people in the portraits actually are, do you? Do the decks come with a list of the subjects?" Faith asked.

"There's a sheet in the box with all the names." She picked up a deck near her open cashbox and slid out the cards. She showed Faith the king of hearts. "This is Charles Huffam, the president of the society." Then she displayed the queen of spades. "Octavia Skimsby. I don't think she holds a specific office in the club."

Faith took the card from the vendor's hand and studied it. Now that she knew who it was meant to be, she could recognize the unpleasant woman's pinched face. "How about the red queens?" she asked.

The vendor fished them out of the deck and held them up. "Caroline Skimsby and Marie de Roux. The artistry is really quite lovely."

"Yes, it is." Faith pulled out the card that matched the one Officer Laddy had found in Mr. Alried's suite. *Why does the woman seem so familiar?* She stared at the picture, trying to match it to any of the society members she'd seen. Then she made the connection. Marie de Roux was the rather short-tempered Frenchwoman she'd spoken to in the first reading, the one who wasn't dressed in Victorian costume.

Faith took her purchases and drifted down to the next vendor, her mind still on the cards. Why would someone leave them as symbols of the thief? Was it to distract the police? Or could it be some kind of threat that only a member of the society would recognize? She felt strongly that the cards were important, if she could just figure out how.

She made sure to peruse the items on every cart and soon added more purchases to her collection. She bought a package of Victorian sweets for Aunt Eileen and an unusual reproduction brooch for her mother. With her winter coat slung over one arm and a number of gifts in the other, she fumbled when her phone began to ring.

It was Brooke. "Are you available to have lunch?" her friend asked. "I know you don't work until this afternoon, so if you're off doing something fun, I completely understand."

"Actually I'm here at the vendor fair," Faith said. "And buying nearly everything I see. Let me unload my purchases in the library and make sure I don't need to tidy up any books and I'll come down. I'd love to eat with you."

Faith nearly dropped her packages again when she reached the library door and unlocked it, but she managed to get the door open and carried her things into the shadowy room. To her surprise, she saw a flash of movement at the terrace windows. Watson stood peering inside, his nose pressed against the glass.

Faith groaned. She crossed to her desk and set down her packages, then headed back to the French doors to let the cat in. "So much for staying home safe and sound," she scolded as she opened the door. "Come on in."

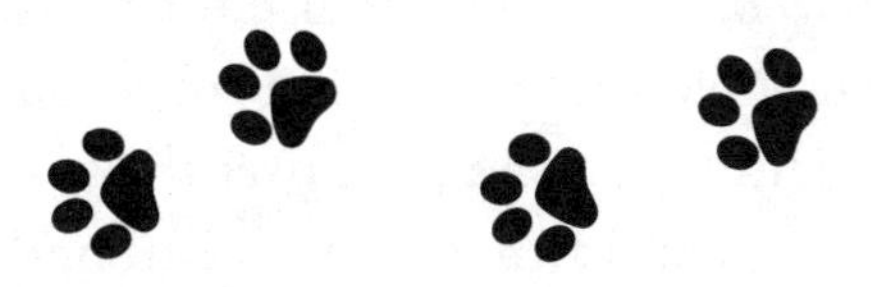

The cat's stub of a tail twitched as he leaned close to the door and sniffed. He knew his human wanted him to rush in, but it was never a good idea to give her what she wanted too quickly. Humans could easily be spoiled. Every cat knew that. Careful training of his beloved human was what had made their long relationship so strong.

Timing was everything. He had to wait long enough to remind her who was in charge. On the other hand, if he waited too long, she might reach down and drag him through the door. That lacked dignity and was completely unacceptable. He stood up and prepared to dart through the door at the first sign of the human bending down, but then something else caught his attention. The sound of a scuffle. Without another thought, the cat turned and raced across the tiled terrace in search of the source.

"Watson!" Faith snapped. "Come back here." For an instant she considered just closing the door and leaving him outside. He'd come back to the door when he got chilly enough. But the memory of the first time she'd ever seen him, a shivering kitten, came to her. She couldn't leave Watson out in the cold now any more than she could then. It was worth a try, anyway.

With an annoyed huff, Faith stalked out on the terrace and closed the library door behind her. Her hand-knit sweater, a gift from her aunt Eileen, was a beautiful shade of gray and wonderfully soft, but the brutal New England wind cut through it like tissue paper, and the light blazer she wore over the sweater didn't add much insulation either. Faith would have to find the cat fast or give up and go back to the library for her coat.

Luckily, she didn't have to look far. She hurried down the terrace stairs and walked around the large bush that bloomed in the spring but was spiky and bare now. As she circled the bush, she saw Watson peeking out from under the far side. Faith crept up on him, hoping to grab the cat before he raced away again. She was so intent on Watson that she didn't immediately note the drama playing out on the garden path ahead. She glanced up, startled, when she heard grunts and muttered curses.

Walden and Charles were in a clinch, gripping each other by lapels and coat sleeves as they struggled. Walden's hair stuck out on his head and his knit hat lay on the ground nearby. The scratches Octavia had given Charles stood out starkly on his cold-whitened cheek.

"Gentlemen!" Faith called out.

Her voice clearly distracted Walden, and his head turned sharply in her direction.

Charles took advantage of his distraction to use his greater weight to knock the younger man to the ground. "Lay hands on me again and you'll be sorry you were born," he growled before pushing past Faith on his way to the manor.

Faith rushed over to the fallen man. "Mr. Garder, are you all right?"

Walden waved off the hand she offered and scrambled to his feet on his own. Faith saw that one of his eyes was already swelling, and she wondered what had happened before she arrived. "I will be fine. Thank you."

"Do you want me to call someone?" Faith was sure his face would soon begin to sprout a rainbow of colors. "Maybe we can get you an ice pack or something. I fear you're going to have a black eye."

Walden smoothed his hair. "No, but you could pretend you didn't witness this. It was not exactly my finest hour, and frankly I'm already ashamed of my behavior. Good day, Miss Newberry. I'm sorry you had to see that side of me." He picked up his hat, tipped it to her, and strode away toward the manor.

Faith stood, watching him, until Watson bumped against her ankles. She bent and scooped up the cat. "I don't know whether to scold you for running off or to thank you for giving me a chance to break that up. This has certainly been an unusual few days. I wonder if the Dickens Society always has such dramatic gatherings."

Watson rubbed his head against her shoulder as she walked back to the library.

The cat had settled down in front of the fire by the time Faith finished checking the library for any misplaced books or immediate needs. Finding nothing, she tiptoed out, leaving Watson napping while she went downstairs to join Brooke for lunch.

Located in the basement, the Castleton Manor kitchen was huge and wonderfully warm compared to the chilly basement hallways. Always bustling with activity, the kitchen reminded Faith of a beehive. At a glance it might look a bit chaotic, but everyone knew exactly what they needed to do.

At the back corner of the kitchen, a small table stood ready for any staff who needed to eat but couldn't walk away and leave the kitchen unattended. It was there that Faith and Brooke settled down for lunch.

"This salad is beautiful," Faith said, raising her voice over the rattle of pots and pans not far away.

"I call it Christmas salad," Brooke said. "The Christmas parts are the turkey, dried cranberries, and roast chestnuts and pecans on a bed of dark greens."

For a few minutes, they settled into the food with only quiet sounds of appreciation. Faith knew Brooke would be busy throughout the day, so it wouldn't be fair if she couldn't actually eat during her lunch hour, but Faith was eager to talk about the strange events since the beginning of the Dickens Society gala.

Brooke pointed at Faith with a forkful of salad. "All right, you're bursting with news. Have you learned something new about these burglaries? Or are you just going to ask me for my help with picking out an outfit for the tree lighting tonight?" She popped the bite into her mouth with a mischievous grin.

"I *am* going to ask you for outfit suggestions," Faith said, "since you know my wardrobe nearly as well as I do. But I wanted to show you something." She slipped her hand into her blazer pocket and took out the deck of cards.

Brooke's eyes widened. "Is that where the card in Mrs. Pugh's room came from?"

"Not this deck specifically," Faith said. "I bought it at the vendor fair this morning. But it came from one just like it." She handed over the deck, and Brooke flipped through it with interest.

She wrinkled her nose as she examined a card. "Charles should have put his face on a joker, not the king."

"His behavior has certainly been anything but royal." She told Brooke about her own encounter with Charles and about his altercations with both Octavia and Walden.

"I'm sorry you had to put up with that creep," Brooke said. "Maybe I got off light by having him *not* want to be involved with my book. I wish I'd seen him get his face scratched. That must have been satisfying."

Faith poked at her salad, her appetite suddenly waning. "It was mostly alarming. We sure aren't seeing much Christmas spirit around here."

"Then let's talk about something cheerier," Brooke said. "I love that sweater. Did Eileen make it?"

Faith smiled. "She did." As the head librarian at the privately funded Candle House Library in the historic downtown of Lighthouse Bay, Faith's aunt loved books as much as Faith herself did, but books weren't Eileen's only passion. She was an amazing knitter, despite the arthritis she lived with every day. This time of year was especially hard, as Faith knew the chill must sink into the joints of her aunt's hands. But Eileen wasn't one to complain.

From the topic of Eileen, they moved on to Faith's wardrobe, and Brooke seemed able to remember every item Faith owned as she debated its suitability as a date outfit. Faith frowned when her friend pooh-poohed the conservative outfit Faith was considering as "not romantic enough."

"I don't need a romantic outfit, because this isn't really a date," Faith said, shaking her head. "It's just two friendly colleagues attending a local event together."

"Like a date," Brooke said.

"Like friends," Faith insisted.

"Gorgeous, rich friends."

"I'm neither gorgeous nor rich."

Brooke grinned. "Not a problem. Wolfe has both in spades. And you are gorgeous. I wouldn't mind having your long legs or your cheekbones."

"You do just fine," Faith said, hoping to deflect the conversation before those cheekbones burst into flames. Though she did rather agree with Brooke's assessment of Wolfe, the whole conversation was overwhelming her. "Back to clothes. How about my gray wool pants? They're nice and warm."

Brooke shook her head. "Date clothes are not chosen for comfort."

"I know. It's not a date." After a little more discussion, they settled on a few possibilities. Faith decided to steer the conversation away from anything that made her blush, so she broached the subject of the Candle House Book Club's upcoming Christmas party.

They talked about the party for a bit, then Brooke had to return to work. "I'm going to think about your outfit for tonight while I cook. Drop by before you leave and I'll have the perfect suggestion."

"I will," Faith agreed. "Thanks."

The lunch had restored Faith's good spirits, and she went back upstairs with more of her regular spring in her step. She was glad to find Watson still curled up in one of the red velvet chairs near the fireplace. "At least you're staying out of trouble," she said to him before turning to her preparations for the dramatic reading.

When the society members began to file in for the reading, Faith noticed they hadn't put on their Victorian finery this time. Most seemed cheerful, and Faith overheard a number of compliments about the resort, the food, and the spa. The positive mood buoyed Faith's spirits even more. Maybe the rest of the event would be transformed by Christmas spirit, just as Scrooge was transformed in *A Christmas Carol*.

Her high hopes were a bit shaken when Walden and Charles arrived in their full Dickensian costumes, both looking a bit worse for wear. Their attitude toward each other seemed professional enough, and they quickly started the reading. The scratches on Charles's cheek were his only visible wound, but Faith noticed he held his mouth oddly and he winced once or twice when he spoke, making it clear that he was in some discomfort. Walden sported an impressive black eye, as Faith had predicted.

Though the two men were dressed mostly the same as they had been during the first reading, Walden had skipped the scarf and chain since he was reading the Ghosts of Christmas Past and Present and neither was the chain-rattling sort. He had brought his dog, but he lay quietly in front of the fire, exchanging doleful expressions with Watson.

Several of the guests had brought their pets, including the woman Faith had spoken with briefly during the first reading, the one whose portrait graced the playing card found at the scene of the second burglary. Marie carried a teacup poodle that trembled in her arms. Faith wondered if the shaking was simply the normal nervous issues with such a small dog or if the poodle was picking up on her mistress's emotions. The dark-haired woman certainly had plenty of attitude, and she stood glaring at Charles.

But she wasn't the only one. Octavia was also scowling at the society president while giving her daughter a rather obvious cold shoulder. Caroline appeared to be oblivious to her mother's behavior, but something was clearly bothering her. She was pale, and her gaze never wavered from the two men speaking.

While she was observing the crowd, Faith felt someone come up beside her. She turned to see Evelyn. The handsome older woman was dressed in an expensive-looking dress that Faith suspected might be cashmere and silk.

"We're not exactly one big happy family here, are we?" Evelyn asked.

"It's not really my place to comment on guests of the manor."

"What fun is there in that?" Evelyn responded. She nodded toward Marie. "Take that one, for instance. Poor thing. She never liked Charles and is now stuck working with him since she was elected treasurer. She's been overtly miserable ever since."

Despite herself, Faith's curiosity was piqued. "Why doesn't she like him?"

Evelyn shrugged. "Who knows? Charles is so very easy to dislike."

Faith had to agree with that, but she decided not to share her thoughts. Instead she tried to ignore the undercurrents in the room and enjoy the reading, which was excellent. Whatever else might be true of the two men, they were skilled performers. Charles seemed a little prone to overacting, but with his striking physical resemblance to Charles Dickens, his posturing actually seemed to work.

When the reading finished, Faith joined the applause around the room. She glanced to her side where Evelyn still stood next to her. Faith suddenly thought of the playing cards she'd purchased earlier in the day. "I discovered where the card in your room originated."

Evelyn raised her eyebrows. "Really? I hadn't given it any more thought."

"It came from a deck of cards commissioned by Mr. Huffam for the Dickens Society. I bought a deck today from one of the vendors."

"That makes sense. I had heard about the project, but I didn't buy a deck and didn't make the connection. I should have."

"Why didn't you buy a deck?" Faith inquired. "They're lovely."

The other woman was interesting. Though extremely friendly toward Faith, Evelyn often seemed a little apart from the society. It was clear everyone knew her by the way they reacted when she moved through the crowd or spoke. The comments by society members made after the burglary made it sound as if they found her boastful about her wealth, but Faith hadn't found that to be true at all.

Evelyn's soft laugh pulled Faith out of her reverie. "Vanity, I suppose. My feelings were hurt because I wasn't asked to pose for any of the cards. I thought maybe Charles thought me too old to model—he does love young women. But then he picked Octavia." She rolled her eyes. "Octavia may like to pretend she's young, but I'd be willing to bet she has nearly ten years on me." She sighed in mock woe. "I have to assume I am simply not one of Charles's favorites."

"But Marie is on one of the cards, and you said she dislikes Mr. Huffam."

Evelyn's laugh was sharp this time. "Who said any of Charles's favorites *like* him?"

Something about the brittle laugh and the starkness of the sentiment sent a chill down Faith's spine.

If Evelyn noticed Faith's reaction, it didn't keep her from continuing with the same line of thought. "I expect every member of the society has wanted to see Charles drop dead at least once."

"Surely not," Faith said.

"As I said, Charles is easy to dislike. It's effortless really. And to indulge in Charles's favorite habit of quoting Dickens, 'He would make a lovely corpse.'"

8

Apparently Charles had noticed Faith and Evelyn conversing during his performance because he gave Faith a disgusted look as he passed by on the way to the refreshment table.

Evelyn merely laughed at him when he tried the same expression on her. "You mustn't let him cow you, Miss Newberry," she said loudly enough that Faith was sure Charles could hear. "Like all predators, if he senses weakness, it only encourages him."

"Thank you for the advice," Faith said, keeping her own voice at a more confidential volume. "You should try the refreshments. The kitchen does a wonderful job."

"I refuse to be chastened, though I will go have a snack. But before I do, tell me honestly. Are the pet treats here good? I want to bring my darling girls a little something, but they are so picky."

"The treats all come from Happy Tails and are baked by a dear friend of mine who is also a skilled vet. Watson loves them," Faith said. "His favorites are the tunaroons, a tuna-flavored macaroon, but Watson loves anything fishy."

"Then I'll bring the girls a present," Evelyn said as she directed her gaze toward the refreshment table. "But first, treats for me."

Faith watched her walk away. She was grateful for Evelyn's friendliness, and the woman was a fountain of information about the society, but she wondered why Evelyn was even *in* the society when she didn't appear to like any of the members.

"Miss Newberry?"

Faith turned to see Walden's battered face. "Yes?"

"I wanted to apologize. I wasn't very gracious earlier today when you were trying to be helpful. I did appreciate your concern."

"It's quite all right. I wasn't offended," Faith said. "I hope you're feeling okay."

"Well, my face is a little sore." He grinned, then winced. "This is definitely a day when a blank expression is more comfortable, but I'll be fine. Do you think the black eye gives me a rakish look?"

Before Faith could respond, Caroline appeared beside them. The young woman pointed at him. "It makes you look like a silly fool who gets into fights."

Walden's eyes widened. "Do tell me exactly how you feel, Miss Skimsby."

"I thought I just did." She crossed her arms over her chest. "I cannot believe you allowed Charles to provoke you into a fistfight."

"There weren't a lot of fists involved," Walden said ruefully. "Even my black eye was more of an elbow. I don't think either of us has a future in professional boxing."

"This is all funny to you?" Caroline's voice grew sharper. She jabbed Walden's chest with a forefinger. "You could have been seriously hurt."

"Some things are worth a little pain," Walden said. "I'm a peaceful man, but sometimes you have to step up. This was one of those times, and I would do it again, though I might duck next time elbows fly."

Something in Walden's tone made Faith think they might prefer to speak privately, so she excused herself and headed for the refreshment table. As she nibbled on a sugarplum, she thought of how glad she'd be when the day was over. The tension between society members was beginning to make her jumpy. The Christmas tree lighting would be something festive and happy to help her get back into a proper holiday mood, assuming she didn't faint with nerves at being there with Wolfe.

At the end of her workday, Faith didn't dawdle over locking up the library. She wanted to have enough time to get dressed, and she still needed to pop downstairs to hear Brooke's final clothes suggestion. She almost considered skipping that to give herself more time to get ready, but she knew she'd feel more secure with a little advice.

Brooke was rushing around the kitchen when Faith came in. "There you are. I have your outfit all sketched out." Brooke hurried over to the back table and snatched up a piece of paper. "I was going to suggest you wear your hair up. You have a gorgeous neck. But it would be wasted on a chilly night with a scarf, so down should be fine."

Faith absorbed the wave of comments. She hadn't even thought about her hair, nor had she ever thought of her neck as "gorgeous." She looked down at the paper Brooke thrust into her hand. "A skirt? Isn't it a little cold for that?"

"Not with boots and leggings. And you have those great boots." Brooke tapped the paper. "This is perfect. Trust me."

"I do." Faith reached out and squeezed her friend's hand. "Thanks for taking time to do this."

"What are friends for? Now don't forget the book club's Christmas party tomorrow night at the library. We'll want to hear all about your date."

Faith sighed. "It's not a date."

"Of course not." Brooke caught the arm of someone carrying a bowl of onions. "Wait. Those need to be chopped." She gave Faith a quick hug. "See you later. Have fun!"

As Faith headed back upstairs, she felt even more antsy than before. She was glad she'd eaten plenty of refreshments after the reading because her nerves had her stomach in knots. "It's just two friends enjoying a public Christmas event," she reminded herself as she scooped up Watson and headed for the doors leading outside. She had decided not to walk through the manor again. She didn't want to risk anyone wanting to stop and chat.

The weather had warmed slightly throughout the day, which was pleasant news for the outdoor event. Still, Faith was glad she was wearing her warm wool coat as she walked to the cottage.

After feeding Watson, Faith went straight to her bedroom, where she quickly tried on the outfit Brooke had recommended. She frowned in the mirror. The deep green sweater had silver threads woven into the yarn that brought out the very faint red tones in her chestnut hair. "It's pretty," Faith told the mirror, "but it feels too dressy."

She changed her clothes several more times, laying the discarded outfits on her bed.

At some point, Watson walked in and hopped up to perch on her pillow and watch the frenzy of changing.

"Oh, Watson," Faith said, exasperated, "I don't know what to wear. What do you think?"

The cat stepped off the pillow and padded over to the deep green sweater. He sniffed it delicately, then sat down beside it.

"You like that one?" Faith asked. "You don't think it's too dressy?"

If the cat thought about it one way or another, it didn't show. He merely blinked at her, then flopped over onto the single bare spot of quilt and closed his eyes.

"Thank you for not shedding on the clothes. I don't blame you for washing your paws of the whole thing," Faith said. She picked the green sweater back up and tried it on again. It was a lovely color, and it was soft and warm. She decided to go with it after all, though she matched it with charcoal wool dress pants instead of the skirt Brooke had recommended. Sometimes comfort had to win.

She'd just finished touching up her lipstick when the phone rang, and she saw it was Wolfe.

He asked her if she'd be willing to meet him at the main house. "I can send a car down to the cottage if you'd like to avoid walking in the cold again," he said. "I'm tied up for another few minutes, but as soon as I finish we can leave from here for the tree lighting."

"I don't mind walking back to the manor," Faith said. "Or should I meet you at the garage?" She knew Wolfe kept his car in the garage along with a small collection of expensive cars that belonged to different family members.

"No, we're not taking my car," Wolfe said. "I thought we'd ride in a horse-drawn carriage. We hired enough to carry everyone in the society to the tree lighting, and I'm sure there will be room for us."

"That does sound like fun," Faith agreed, though she sincerely hoped they wouldn't have to sit with any of the more trying members of the society. "I'm leaving now."

As his human wrapped herself in the things she used to make up for her sad lack of fur, the cat watched her attentively. She was upset by something. He didn't like seeing his human upset. And he didn't intend to let her go out alone while she was distressed. She always seemed to get herself into trouble when he left her alone for too long.

When his human opened the front door, he was ready, having slunk along behind her, nearly close enough to touch her with a whisker but careful not to. He was able to time his exit through the door exactly with hers, and he darted under a bush before she noticed him. He would follow from a distance and jump in only if needed.

To the cat's disgust, once his human reached the big house, she climbed into a large wheeled carriage that stood along the front of the building. Each carriage was pulled by stamping, snorting, stinking horses. Did she have no sense at all? The cat couldn't leave her alone in such a dangerous situation. He leaped up beside the carriage driver's feet and ducked under the bench, hunching down to wait for the nightmare to end.

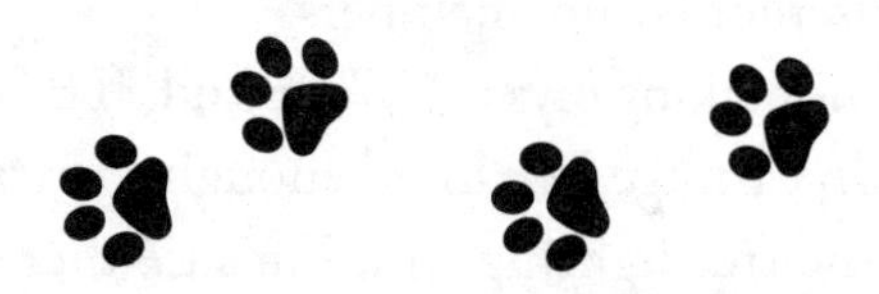

As the horses pulled the carriage down the long drive, Faith felt the stresses of the day fall away behind her. Judging by the way his knee jiggled beside her, Wolfe was nearly as excited as the little boy who sat across from them. Faith learned he was the son of one of the manor employees, and Wolfe had invited the boy and his mother along after hearing the boy begging his mother to take him.

"Mom says the tree is fifty feet tall," the boy informed them. "How do they get the lights all the way to the top?"

"They use a crane," Wolfe told him. "When I was your age, I enjoyed watching the crane almost as much as the tree lighting itself. I would ride my bike into town to watch the lights go on the tree and imagine being up in that crane, and then I came back with my whole family for the lighting."

"Riding in the crane would be cool," the boy said.

Faith could tell Wolfe sincerely agreed. She liked seeing this side of her employer. Wolfe was so busy with the demands of Castleton Manor and his family's other properties that Faith wondered how often he let himself relax. She was glad he'd taken the time tonight.

"Faith, are you warm enough?" he asked.

"I'm fine. My coat is very thick." And sitting next to her boss made her feel positively flushed. She hoped he would attribute her pink cheeks to the cold.

When they reached downtown Lighthouse Bay, the carriages pulled to a stop in a line near where the tree lighting was to take place. Wolfe hopped out of the carriage and held out his hand to help Faith down. As her foot touched the pavement, her attention was drawn to a flash of movement. From the front of the carriage a familiar stumpy-tailed, black-and-white cat jumped to the ground.

"Watson!" Faith exclaimed.

The cat looked back at her and took one step toward her. Then the carriage driver hopped down directly beside him, startling the cat. Watson's fur stood out in a puff, and he raced away.

"Watson!" Faith yelled and ran after him.

"Faith?" Wolfe called.

"I'll be right back," she replied without turning around. Faith didn't know if Wolfe had heard her, but she didn't dare stop or even take her eyes off the cat. He was so small that he could disappear into the crowd in the blink of an eye.

Watson was clearly spooked and Faith feared he would dash out into the street or under the hooves of the horses. Instead, the cat darted across the green, weaving between the legs of the crowd.

Faith followed Watson as closely as she could, but she eventually lost him in the maze of people. She stood near the edge of the big pine tree, panting softly and scanning the area for any sign of the cat.

Wolfe came up beside her, his own quickened breathing suggesting he must have run after her. "I've had trouble with being stood up before," he said, "but I've never had a date run away from me. That might be a new low."

Faith startled at the word *date. Surely he's just being humorous.* Still a little out of breath, she explained about Watson.

"Are you sure it was him?" Wolfe asked. "Maybe the carriage driver owns a cat."

"A cat with a stumpy tail and tuxedo markings? That would be awfully coincidental," Faith said. "Watson responded when I called his name. I'm certain it was him. And I'm worried about him in this crowd."

"Watson is very competent," Wolfe said. "I'm sure he'll be fine. He'll probably be in the carriage when we get back to it."

Not wanting to ruin Wolfe's time, Faith tried to sound like she believed it when she agreed with him. She reminded herself of the times Watson had made his way home from fairly far away. The cat was definitely resourceful.

They stood together as the festivities surrounding the tree lighting began. The high school band launched into a selection of Christmas music with more enthusiasm than skill.

When the band finished several songs, the mayor approached the microphone and began telling the crowd some history of the town.

Faith loved anything about history and would have hung on every word, but she spotted a black-and-white head peeking out at her from one of the lower branches of the huge tree. She silently slipped away from Wolfe and headed for Watson.

The cat hopped down from the branch and trotted around toward the back of the tree.

Faith followed him, hissing, "Watson, come here right now."

Compared with the crowd at the other side of the tall tree, this area was empty. No one stood at the back side of the tree. The branches blocked the view of the band and other performers and even muffled the sound. With that in mind, Faith raised her voice. "Watson, get back here or you won't get another Happy Tails treat for the rest of the year." She considered saying, "for the rest of your life," but she wanted him to consider believing her.

Watson paused and peered in her direction as if trying to figure out whether she was bluffing. Then he ducked under the tree.

Faith bent over and followed him. In the deep shadows under the enormous tree, she found Watson sniffing a shiny black boot.

Someone lay sprawled and unmoving under the tree.

Most of the person's body was obscured by the darkness near the trunk of the tree. Immediately Faith thought of some of the homeless people she'd seen sheltering in unlikely places in cities. Certainly Lighthouse Bay would have a better place for the poor man to get out of the cold. "Sir," she said, "are you all right?"

As Faith crept closer, she noticed a large dark stain on the man's coat, and she realized the man was not all right. And he would never be all right again.

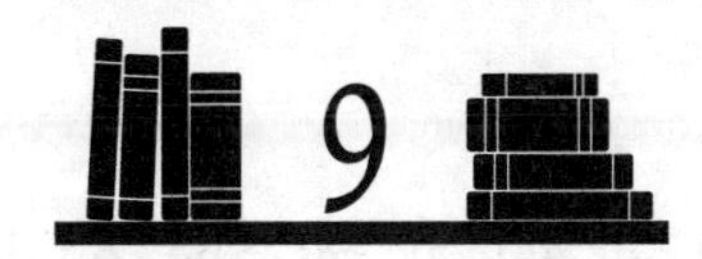

9

Surrounded by darkness, Faith jerked herself out of the troubling dream she'd been having and sat up. She reached over to turn on the lamp next to the bed and noticed Watson had deserted her. She supposed he hadn't appreciated her excessive tossing and turning.

She shuddered as she remembered what had prompted her restless night and wrapped her arms around herself, trying to blot out the image of Charles lying under that tree.

It had taken the police no time to determine Charles's death was murder—lacerations and blunt-force trauma. At least that was what the police chief told Wolfe as Faith stood clinging to Watson. Though the police had searched the underside of the tree thoroughly, they had found no sign of the actual murder weapon. Charles's lack of popularity with the people in the Charles Dickens Society was obvious, but Faith couldn't imagine who could dislike him enough to kill him.

She swung her legs over the side of the bed and looked at her alarm clock. It was hours before she needed to get up, but the idea of returning to the nightmares had no appeal so she pushed her feet into her faux fur-lined slippers and scuffed out to the kitchen.

From there she could see Watson curled up in her chair by the fire. "Deserter," she muttered, then turned to get the coffee started.

Today was definitely going to be a strong coffee day. Most of the society had been at the tree lighting, but no details had been released about the murder victim, so everyone would be clamoring to find out who it was. She couldn't imagine what would happen when the society learned it was their president.

When Watson insisted upon dashing out of the cottage with her later, she didn't have the heart to hustle him back inside. Faith had plenty of experience to know the futility of that. Instead, she hunched her shoulders against the early-morning chill and forced herself toward the manor.

As she walked, she thought about the people she knew who had a problem with Charles. She'd already given Walden's and Octavia's names to Chief Garris. She'd actually seen both of them get physical with Charles.

The other names on her mental list were more nebulous. She knew nothing about why Marie hated Charles, but she believed the woman did, and she knew Evelyn also had some kind of problem with the man, though she hardly seemed to have strong enough feelings to kill anyone. Caroline appeared displeased by Charles's attentions toward her, but Faith didn't like the man's smarmy "flirting" either, so she didn't consider that much of a murder motive.

Not to mention Brooke was still angry about Charles's reaction to her asking him about her book, but Faith knew without question that her friend would never kill anyone. And the idea that she'd murder someone over a cookbook or because she'd been chewed out by Marlene was ludicrous.

Faith was so caught up in turning the names over in her head that the walk to the manor house seemed unusually short, even with the frigid air blowing in from the water. She slipped inside and headed for the library with Watson at her heels. As soon as she started down the gallery, she saw a crowd milling around the library doors, and she had a sinking feeling that they weren't all eager for a good book to read.

"Good morning," she said, then winced. A man had died the night before. It wasn't really a very good morning.

"Is it true?" Marie demanded. "Did you find Charles's body last night?"

"I need to open the library," Faith replied, searching for a way through the small crowd without being impolite.

But Marie planted herself directly in Faith's path. "Is it true?" she repeated, peering into Faith's face.

"It's true. And it was terrible. I would prefer not to talk about it," Faith replied firmly.

"Only one more question," Marie said. "Was it murder?"

"The police believe it was."

Marie stepped out of Faith's way, and the rest of the group parted to let her through. Faith opened the library door and went inside. Her usual sense of contentment as she entered the beautiful library was dulled by the prying crowd behind her, but she still felt better. Watson padded over to take his place on a chair near the fire, though Faith saw that he watched her carefully despite his relaxed pose.

Faith turned to smile at the group that had followed her in. She was glad to see some of the people had turned away at the door, including Marie. Just hearing the confirmation of Charles's murder seemed to be enough. The others spread out, browsing the library shelves, but Faith noticed they managed to slip in questions about the murder whenever she got close.

By midmorning, the combination of poor sleep and questions for which she had no answers left Faith with a pounding headache, but the society had a morning tea on the schedule and apparently it wasn't canceled. The library emptied as the members headed to the salon for tea. Faith watched the last of them walk out and realized that although the society members who'd come in were clearly shocked and luridly curious, not a one of them seemed even marginally sad about the death of Charles.

Faith had just pulled Watson into her lap and settled into a chair near the fire to take a small breather when Police Chief Andy Garris walked in. The tall, well-built former marine held his fur-trimmed winter hat in his hand. "I know last night must have been hard," he said gently, "but I have a few more questions."

Faith started to rise from her chair, but the chief waved her back down and took a seat nearby. "We might as well enjoy the fire."

"It's one of the perks of the job," Faith said as she sat back and stroked Watson's fur. "There's always a fire waiting for me when I come in."

"That's a nice setup." He removed a notebook from his pocket and flipped through the pages. "I've seen the playing cards found at the scenes of the burglaries. Could you tell me where exactly you found the first one?"

"You think the playing cards are connected to the murder?"

"Possibly. We found bits of the king of spades torn up and strewn across Mr. Huffam's body."

Faith hadn't noticed that, but the area under the tree had been dark and she'd scrambled away as soon as she realized she was looking at a dead man. "So the burglar may have killed him?"

"It's confusing. When we searched the victim's room this morning, we found all the missing property rolled into a pair of socks in a drawer. It certainly seems he was connected with the burglaries in some way."

"But Charles physically could not have been the burglar," Faith said. "He was performing when it happened. I was witness to it, as were the rest of the society members."

"I know," the chief said, his voice patient, "but clearly Mr. Huffam was involved. So I'm thinking the murder may have been a falling-out between thieves. Where exactly did you find the first card?"

"I didn't. Watson found it. I told Officer Laddy the details."

"There weren't many details in his report. I need you to concentrate. Did you see which direction Watson came from before you noticed he had the card?"

Faith closed her eyes and tried to replay the events. "It may have been along the wall, maybe even near the window. I believe he came from that direction. But you know, if the card interested Watson, it might have been moved from the original spot by Evelyn's cats."

"I understand that, but now that we have a murder, I want to be certain we track down every detail," Chief Garris explained. "Were you aware that Mr. Huffam had a prior relationship with your boss Ms. Russell?"

The question was so out of the blue that Faith was caught off guard, but she racked her brain for any related information. "Actually I do think Charles said something about having known Marlene for a while. But I never saw them together. You can't think Marlene has anything to do with his death?"

"This is a complicated case. I'm exploring all possibilities," Garris said. "And Ms. Russell does have a history of being manipulated by unscrupulous men to do rather unfortunate things. Her past situation was not so terribly different from this one."

"But she didn't kill anyone," Faith protested. Marlene hadn't even gone to jail for the things she'd done in the past, though Faith had heard she had to do some community service. Her prickly boss certainly didn't chat with her about it.

"No, she didn't." The chief closed his notebook and stared into the fire for a few minutes.

Faith sat still. She hoped the chief wouldn't hear about Brooke's cookbook. If he was considering Marlene a suspect, he'd certainly look askance at Brooke, who'd been visibly furious with Charles about his casual dismissal of her and the way he'd gotten her into trouble with Marlene.

"Charles wasn't a very popular man," Faith said.

"So I've learned. It makes you wonder how he became the president of the society. It's an elected position. Why would the membership elect someone most of them disliked so thoroughly?"

"I don't know."

"Neither do I." Chief Garris frowned. "But I'm very interested to know, so I think I'll keep poking until I find out." He leaned over and scratched Watson on the head. "It was this rascal who led you to the victim's body, right?"

"I don't think he did it on purpose," Faith said. "He wasn't supposed to be in town, and he probably knew I was going to haul him home. The tree was just a good potential hiding place."

"Still, he's found two important clues to this case. I don't want to encourage you to interfere with an investigation, but you be sure to let me know if you find anything else . . . or if he does."

"I will, Chief."

Garris hauled himself from the chair, nodded to Faith, and left the library.

Faith stood and settled Watson back into the chair. "I need to do some straightening," she said. "Half the people in here this morning weren't the slightest bit interested in reading, and they still managed to leave books unshelved."

Watson blinked at her, clearly unmoved by her grumbling.

She walked around, putting the library in order and enjoying the silence of the huge room. The only sounds came from the crackling of the fireplace.

As she shelved the last of the misplaced items, Faith decided to use what was left of the quiet time to catalog some new books

Wolfe had bought for the library after his last trip to Europe, ones he thought might interest the guests. She smiled, thinking it was just one more bit of proof that he was a thoughtful man.

"Miss Newberry?"

Faith turned to see a big man who held his broad shoulders in a slump that matched the mildly nervous expression on his face.

The man showed her a thick leather-bound book. "I borrowed this book from the library on the night of the first reading. It's my favorite of Dickens's works." He flipped open the book. "Are you aware of this inscription?"

Faith examined the flyleaf of the copy of *Great Expectations*. The paper in the book had yellowed with the years, and the ink used to pen an inscription had faded a bit over time, but the spidery handwriting was still readable: *For Wilfred. You'll always be Pip to me. Love, Martita.*

"Do you know if that inscription was written by Martita Hunt?" he asked. "She played Miss Havisham in the movie version of *Great Expectations* in the 1940s."

"I don't actually know. I can ask Mr. Jaxon. Most of the older books in our collection have belonged to his family for quite some time. I suspect the Wilfred mentioned in the inscription may be one of the Jaxons."

"I'd love to know what you find out," the man said, his expression eager. "My mother was a movie buff, and I saw that version of *Great Expectations* when I was a boy. Miss Havisham scared me silly. I love the idea of having held a book in my hand that she held in hers."

"If you'll let me borrow back the book for a while, I will ask Mr. Jaxon about this and tell you what I find out, Mister . . ." Faith paused, realizing she didn't know the identity of the man in front of her.

"I'm so sorry. Where are my manners?" The man offered his hand. "My name is Morton Alried."

Now it was Faith's turn to stammer. She wondered if the man had heard about Charles's connection to the burglaries. "I'm pleased to meet you. Let me say how very sorry I am that your cuff links were stolen."

Mr. Alried bobbed his head shyly. "Thank you. Actually I heard from the police earlier. They believe they have recovered my collection, though they haven't caught the culprit yet." He sighed. "I imagine my poor cuff links will be tied up as evidence for rather a long while."

"I'm sure the police will take good care of them."

"I hope so. Thank you for agreeing to research the inscription in the book for me, Miss Newberry. I look forward to hearing what you learn about it. If it is from Miss Hunt, perhaps Mr. Jaxon would consider selling me the book."

"I can certainly ask him. It is an interesting mystery. I hope we can find the answer."

Mr. Alried thanked her again, then excused himself and left Faith alone with the heavy volume in her hand. She had just pulled out her phone to call Wolfe about the book when the library door flung open and Marlene burst in, her face even more pinched than usual.

"What's the matter?" Faith asked. She suspected she knew and Marlene confirmed her suspicion immediately.

"Chief Garris accosted me in my office," Marlene said. "He asked me about my previous relationship with Charles, and I got the distinct impression he considers me a suspect in that man's murder. It's the most ridiculous thing I've ever heard."

"I'm sure the chief is just being thorough," Faith said. "And you did know Mr. Huffam."

"Barely. I went out with him a few times before I met my ex-husband. Thankfully I was a better judge of character with Charles than with my ex. It was long ago and of little importance, but Chief Garris seems fixated on it. I would prefer he didn't waste his time and mine with illogical theories." Marlene folded her arms across her chest. "Normally I disapprove of your habit of meddling in police business, but I believe this may be the exception."

Faith frowned. *I do not meddle in police business.* Her preference was to do her job and stay completely out of police business. It wasn't her fault that these situations were forced on her time after—

"Faith!" Marlene shouted, making Faith jump. "Do I have your attention?"

"Mine and probably the attention of every person on this floor of the manor."

Marlene dropped her volume minimally. "I am concerned that the police will convince themselves that I am somehow involved in this distasteful mess. I do not intend to be arrested, so I expect you to figure out who really killed Charles. Then the police can let me focus on my job here at the manor."

"You honestly want me to track down a murderer?" Faith said, the absurdity of the request making her reel. "Why is it my responsibility?"

"Because you're so good at being nosy and because I am your boss. If you value your job, you'll find the real killer—immediately!"

10

Though she doubted Marlene could fire her even if she wanted to, at least without some cooperation by the Jaxons, Faith could sympathize with Marlene's fears. After ranting for a few more minutes about the inconvenience of being questioned and the unacceptability of being a murder suspect, Marlene left Faith to "get on with investigating."

"How am I supposed to do that?" Faith whispered after Marlene marched out.

She sat down at her desk and fiddled with the book Morton Alried had given her, but her mind was not on the book or the inscription in it. Marlene's demands had her thoughts whirling. There were so many people angry with Charles. How could she pick one to investigate? Then she thought of the chief's question. How *could* a man so universally disliked become president of the Charles Dickens Society? The answer to that might be enlightening, and Faith knew one person who always seemed eager to enlighten her.

Faith decided to head back to the salon to see if Evelyn might be having tea. She was halfway to the door when Octavia swept into the library in full Victorian mourning wearing a veil and a dress as black as a raven's wing.

"Miss Newberry," Octavia said, drawing out the words, "I trust you know about my dearest Charles."

Faith stared. It appeared Octavia was the only person who didn't know Faith had found Charles's body. "Yes, I'm sorry for your loss."

"'Life is made of ever so many partings welded together.'"

That sounded vaguely familiar. "Dickens?"

"And so sadly apropos. I came to tell you that I have met with key members of the society. We have decided to continue the gala, sad though we are, and to continue the reading of *A Christmas Carol*. I believe it is what Charles would want."

"I see," Faith said.

"I will read Charles's part in his honor," Octavia announced. "We will hold the reading just before the dinner hour, so we won't need refreshments of any sort, unless the kitchen would like to do some sort of hors d'oeuvres. We are completely flexible on that." She added the last sentence with the largesse of a queen granting a great favor.

"I'm not really connected to the kitchen. You might want to speak with Marlene Russell about that sort of change, as she coordinates all the different parts of the manor."

A moue of distaste appeared on Octavia's face behind the fine veil. "I find that woman quite unpleasant. Still, I suppose leadership must deal with all sorts of people. I shall speak with her."

"Leadership?" Faith echoed.

"I am acting president of the society."

"I thought Mr. Garder was vice president. Wouldn't he step up to lead the society?" Faith asked, bewildered.

Octavia gave her a withering sneer. "I would not expect you to understand the complexities of the Charles Dickens Society. Suffice it to say that I am empowered to speak for the group since my darling Charles cannot."

Faith stared at her silently, not completely sure how to respond at first. Finally, she said, "I'm glad you and Mr. Huffam made up."

"Pardon me?" Octavia's eyebrows rose in confusion.

"You seemed upset with him when last I saw you. And I couldn't help but notice the scratches on his face."

"My family has always been made up of passionate people," Octavia said. "But like a summer storm, anger blows away quickly. Charles and I could never stay angry with each other for long. We were soul mates." She laughed, the sound forced and brittle. "Charles was only a man. And like any man, he was prone to eyeing every bit of fluff that came along." She looked rather pointedly at Faith.

Faith didn't know if she was amused or offended at being called "fluff," though she kept a professional face. "You're very charitable."

"All the good I am came from being with Charles, and we will honor him for the wonderful man he was."

Octavia prattled on about the reading and changes that would have to be made to the positioning of the library furniture so she could stand farther away from the fireplace. "Such a large fire is quite noisy," she said. "And I don't have Charles's beautiful deep voice that carries, though I will do my best." She sniffed delicately. "For Charles."

Faith had to agree that Octavia's voice was certainly different from Charles's. Octavia's voice had a tendency to screech unpleasantly. She wondered how the older woman had convinced the society to let her do the reading. Again she suspected there were things going on under the surface that she wasn't privy to. She consented to all of Octavia's changes, hoping to move her along so she could slip away to speak with Evelyn, but by the time the older woman wound down on her demands, the tea must have been over. Other members drifted into the library.

The new arrivals had actual questions about book preservation and Victorian bookbinding techniques, so Faith was soon caught up in the discussions. She missed lunch without even noticing it. There were few things she loved discussing more than old books.

The first visitors were followed by a pair of women who wanted advice on some light reading.

One of the women pushed her thick glasses up on her nose. "I had planned to reread *The Mystery of Edwin Drood*, but it's really rather eerie, and with the disquieting death of Charles—well, I think I could use some happy bedtime reading instead."

"I can understand that," Faith said. "Especially since Dickens never finished the book."

"Yes," the woman said. "I hope we're not facing another unsolvable mystery. So I would like to read something bright and cheerful. Something that gives me hope."

"Me too." The second woman handed a murder mystery over to Faith. "I checked this out yesterday, but I don't think it is appropriate reading in light of . . . well . . . things."

Faith gave the women several book suggestions as she led them through the shelves. "I really didn't know Mr. Huffam very well," she said, pointing out a couple of books, "but I'm very sorry for your loss."

"Thank you, dear," the woman with the glasses said. "I didn't actually know Charles particularly well myself." She and her friend exchanged glances and tittered. "We didn't have the money, looks, or youth to get much of Charles's attention."

"For which I'm grateful," her friend said. "I don't like to speak ill of the dead, but Charles was too slick for my taste."

"I actually have met several people who weren't overly fond of him," Faith said. "I'm a little amazed that he was president considering he didn't seem too popular."

"I didn't vote for him," the woman with the glasses said. "And other than poor silly Octavia, I've never heard anyone speak fondly of him. But clearly he had his fans."

"At least during the election," her friend said.

"Maybe it was temporary mass insanity and only we were spared." The woman giggled and pushed her glasses up. "Thank you so much for the help with the books. I believe I'll sit for a while in front of your lovely fire and start reading mine."

"That's an excellent idea, Helen," her friend said, and they hurried over to do just that.

Fortunately Watson had given up his spot on the chair earlier and now sat near the French doors, staring out at the terrace.

Faith glanced down at her watch. There was no way she had time to track down Evelyn before the reading, and she had the book club Christmas party right after work. *Sorry, Marlene,* she thought, *I'll have to wait until tomorrow to follow your command to be nosy.*

When the dramatic reading began, Faith stood near the back of the audience, holding Watson and watching for Evelyn's arrival. She could get in a quick question during the reading, since she doubted Evelyn would be riveted by Octavia's melodramatics, complete with oddly timed hand waving and abundant deep sighs. However, Evelyn still had not shown up when Octavia reached the point in the story where Scrooge had to face his own tombstone. The older woman broke down and sobbed her way unintelligibly through the lines.

In exasperation, Caroline pushed her way through the listeners and took hold of her mother's arm. "That's enough for today," she said. "No one can understand what you're saying anyway."

Octavia pulled back, wailing, "I need to finish for Charles!"

Caroline turned an imploring face toward Walden. He took Octavia's other arm. "Charles would understand," he said. "He would appreciate how hard this is for you."

Faith saw Caroline roll her eyes at his words.

But Octavia sniffled and said, "Do you think he's watching this?"

"Charles never liked to miss anything," Walden said. "Let's get you something to drink." He and Caroline led Octavia through the crowd and over to the refreshment table.

The audience looked at one another for a moment, and then weak applause broke out.

"Thank you. I know you all miss him too," Octavia said, her words punctuated by sobs.

Faith heard a snort beside her and turned to see Marie, who stood close by, holding her small poodle and watching Octavia closely.

"You don't think they miss him?" Faith whispered to her.

Faith's comment drew the attention of the woman's little poodle, who wriggled in her arms and sniffed at Watson.

In disgust, Watson jumped out of Faith's arms and stalked away to sit under Faith's desk.

"I doubt even Octavia truly does," Marie said quietly as she stroked the wiggling dog. "Certainly her daughter does not. Now that she doesn't have to be polite to Charles for her mother's sake, nothing stands between her and her heart's desire."

"What is Caroline's heart's desire?" Faith asked.

"You've got eyes."

Faith turned back to study Caroline, who stood with her hand on her mother's arm as Walden brought the older woman a glass of punch. Caroline and Walden exchanged glances, and Faith immediately realized what Marie meant. Caroline and Walden were definitely involved in some way. The chemistry between them was obvious now that Faith was paying attention to it. But how had Charles stood in the way of that?

"I don't understand. I never saw Caroline show any interest in Charles."

"Her interest in him wasn't the problem. It was his interest in her. Charles was never an easy man to say no to."

"Why is that?" Faith asked.

Marie didn't answer. She merely gave Faith a mysterious half smile instead. "Please excuse me. The hors d'oeuvres look so good, and I think my dog would like a snack." She turned and walked over to the refreshment table.

Faith considered following her, but one of the other guests caught her and began praising the manor and its sensitive handling of a difficult time.

It wasn't until the society members started to file out for dinner that Faith managed to catch Walden alone. "How are you feeling?" she asked.

The gaze he turned toward her was puzzled. "Fine?"

"I thought you might be a little sore." She pointed toward his still-colorful facial bruises.

He laughed and reached up to touch it gingerly. "Maybe a little, though it's not too bad."

"What were you and Mr. Huffam fighting about?"

Walden's tone cooled considerably. "Thank you for your concern about my injury, but I prefer to keep my private life private if it's all the same to you."

"That's a good way to live," Faith said. "If a little challenging in this tell-everything world we live in."

"All the more reason to avoid idle gossip. Good evening, Miss Newberry." He gave her a very clear look, then turned and walked out of the library.

Once the room was empty of everyone except the housekeeping staff, Faith coaxed Watson out from under the desk and carried him to the gallery. She paused to study the statue of Agatha Christie. "How did you make this sleuthing sound so easy? You always knew where to lead your characters next."

If Agatha had an answer, she wasn't sharing.

11

"Did you say these are miniature plum puddings?" Midge Foster asked, turning a tiny fruit-filled cake around in her fingers.

The Chihuahua in her lap eyed the confection with mild interest, eyes huge behind the prescription doggy glasses he wore. Midge brought Atticus to every meeting, a tradition that had disgruntled Watson at first, but the cat had adapted to the friendly little dog, mostly by blatantly ignoring him.

"I adapted a Victorian recipe. I thought they'd be fun," Brooke explained. Her gloomy tone made it sound as if she didn't find anything fun at present.

"They're delicious," Faith said, hoping to cheer her friend up. Brooke had been uncharacteristically quiet and solemn during the entire Candle House Library Book Club Christmas party so far. "You made these for one night of the dramatic readings, didn't you? I loved them then too."

Brooke nodded. "Everyone at the reading ate them up, so I knew I had a winner and wanted to share them with you all." Her voice cracked at the end of the sentence and then dropped to a whisper as she added, "My family."

"Brooke, what's wrong?" Eileen Piper's voice was kind but firm. Brooke had deflected all efforts to get her to talk about what was bothering her, but few people could resist Eileen's gentle tone. For once, Faith's aunt was attending a club meeting without a pile of knitting in her lap. Faith hoped it wasn't because Eileen's arthritis was acting up.

Brooke blinked rapidly, her eyes glassy, then said, "The police think I killed someone."

Everyone in the room gasped.

Faith reached out and took her friend's hand. "I'm sure they don't."

"Chief Garris came down to the kitchen today and asked me all kinds of questions about my *altercation* with Charles. Altercation! You'd think I punched the man in the nose instead of just asking him if he wanted to see my cookbook."

"They think you killed someone because you told him about a cookbook?" Midge's voice reflected her confusion at such an absurd idea.

"Not exactly." Brooke sniffled and grabbed a tissue from a nearby box. "They think I killed him because he ratted me out to Marlene and she threatened to fire me. I was angry about it and not exactly quiet about how mad I was. Now they'll fire me for sure, since I'm a murder suspect."

"That's not likely to happen. Chief Garris is just checking up on everyone even slightly connected with Mr. Huffam," Faith insisted.

"I wish I could be sure of that," Brooke said.

"Be sure," Faith told her. "I spoke with Marlene this afternoon. She is also afraid she's about to be arrested for the murder."

"What?" Brooke gaped.

"Marlene came to the library today and demanded I solve Charles Huffam's murder because she believes the police will pin it on her. Apparently she was also questioned."

"If I had to pick Marlene or Brooke as a potential murderer, I know who I'd choose," Midge said. She nibbled on the edge of her plum pudding. "It wouldn't be Brooke."

"The police don't have any shortage of potential murderers," Faith said as she sat back and rubbed Watson's ears. Constant attention had proved to be the key to keeping Watson out of mischief at meetings. "I don't think Chief Garris seriously believes you might have killed Huffam."

"He was scary enough," Brooke said, though her posture relaxed a little. "And if I had to be grilled by the police, why couldn't it be by that cute Bryan Laddy? I could have enjoyed that."

"I've been questioned by Officer Laddy before. It's not that much fun," Faith admitted. "I honestly don't know how to do what Marlene wants. How am I supposed to track down a murderer before we all scatter for Christmas?"

"You're not," her aunt said decisively. "You just do your job until Christmas break and then go home, visit family, and forget all this. In fact, that's what both of you should do. The police are very competent in Lighthouse Bay. They'll sort it out."

"Normally I would be all for that," Faith said, "but I suspect Marlene is going to want updates on my progress. So I *will* have to do something."

"Just don't do anything dangerous," Midge said. She popped the last of her plum pudding into her mouth.

"Maybe I could help," Brooke offered. "If the police find the killer, they'll stop suspecting me, so it would be a win-win."

Eileen frowned. "I still think you should leave it alone."

"I'll just have a chat with Evelyn Pugh," Faith said. "She's a member of the society and loves gossip. I've already been spending time with her since she has two tailless cats and likes Watson to come visit. I'll pop by and talk with her some more so I'll have something to report to Marlene."

"I suppose that would be all right," Eileen agreed hesitantly.

"Don't worry. I have no intention of getting myself into any dangerous situations." Faith patted her aunt's arm.

Midge snorted softly. When Faith looked at her, she shrugged. "Sorry. I thought you were kidding in light of past behavior."

"I don't put myself in dangerous situations," Faith protested. "It just happens."

"Well, try not to let it happen this time," Eileen urged. "If you don't get home in one piece, I know your mother will blame me for not taking care of you."

"I'm a grown adult," Faith said with a laugh. "I'm remarkably capable of taking care of myself."

"On the topic of grown adults," Brooke said with a mischievous grin, "tell us about your date with Wolfe."

"Date?" Eileen and Midge echoed together, turning wide eyes on Faith.

"It wasn't a date," Faith insisted. "Wolfe just wanted to go to the tree lighting and he asked me along."

"Isn't that what a date is, by definition?" Midge asked.

"We were two friendly coworkers attending a community event."

"And I hope it was *very* friendly," Brooke teased.

"Considering that the second we got out of the carriage, Watson appeared and I chased him around until I found a dead body, the whole event would have to go down in the annals of bad dates, if it was a date. But it wasn't."

"After such a horrible experience, I hope Wolfe saw you home," Eileen said.

"He did. He even insisted on walking me to the cottage and getting me a cup of tea before he left."

"Like a friendly coworker," Brooke said lightly.

Faith frowned at her. "Exactly like a friendly coworker. I seem to remember you doing very similar sorts of things after I was nearly trampled by horses a couple of months ago."

"Enough squabbling," Midge interrupted. "Time for presents!"

Atticus barked his agreement with that idea.

For the rest of the party, the club managed to avoid any more mentions of murder or dating, so Faith relaxed and enjoyed herself.

She was still steeped in Christmas spirit later as she carried Watson out of the library. Streetlights softened the darkness around the beautiful stone building that housed the library. It had once been an actual candle factory, so the outside of the building was simple in design, without any of the lavish adornment of Castleton Manor. Faith paused on the stone patio outside the door to let her eyes adjust to the darkness.

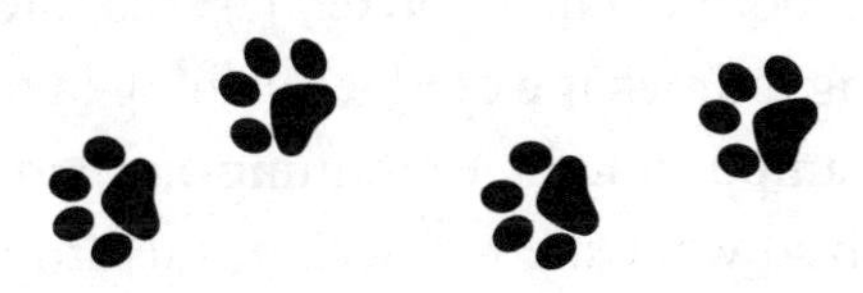

The cat poked his nose over his human's arm and sniffed the chilly night air. He smelled something unusual. The sharp coppery smell wouldn't be ignored. He squirmed once, then leaped out of his human's arms. As soon as he hit the cold stones of the patio, he was running, chasing the mysterious scent.

His human called after him, but every cat knows the demands of humans should be considered suggestions at best. He kept in the shadows to make it harder for his human to locate and catch him. He had to find what was giving off the smell that grew stronger with every bound.

Finally, the cat reached a boxwood hedge that ran alongside one of the town's small visitor parking lots. The smell was definitely coming from the hedge, so he dove inside. That's when he discovered the source. He thrashed the stump of his tail as he realized his human would want to see this.

Faith reached the boxwood hedge, her lungs aching from the frigid night air. "Watson, come out of there," she huffed.

Watson merely meowed in reply.

Faith squatted down and thrust her hand into the hedge, feeling for the cat's soft fur. Instead her fingers touched something cold, hard, and sticky. Curious, she pulled it out into the pool of light from the streetlamp overhead.

The heavy length of chain looked just like the one from the dramatic reading, but what would it be doing in town? She held it closer to the lamppost light, examining one end that was dark. When she realized what she was seeing, she dropped the chain in shock.

She stared down at the blood-covered chain. She had almost certainly just found the weapon that had been used to murder Charles Huffam.

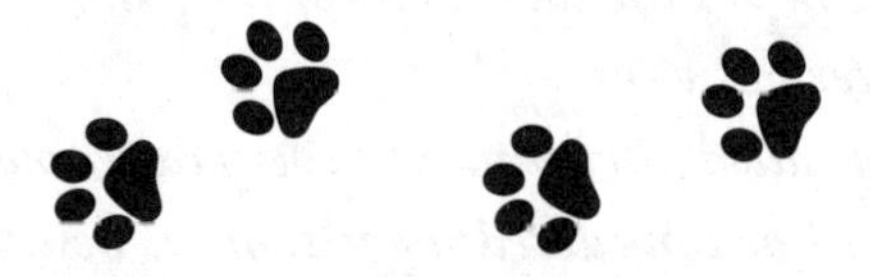

Faith lifted the soft, rose-colored scarf from the gift bag she'd left on the end of her dresser and tried to recapture the happy feeling she'd had when she opened the gift. She'd been so glad Eileen had been the one to draw her name, because her aunt always made the most amazing things. Faith slipped the scarf around her neck and pressed the warmth of the delicate yarn against her skin. She'd felt chilled ever since she'd found the murder weapon the previous evening.

Pushing the gruesome thought from her mind, she peered in the mirror over the dresser and saw that the yarn her aunt had chosen helped brighten her pale cheeks.

As she admired her gift, Watson hopped up onto the dresser and batted at the end of the scarf.

Faith lifted it out of his reach. "You leave this one alone. You've done enough lately."

Watson gazed up at her innocently, and she scowled at him. She'd spent well over an hour out in the cold answering Officer Laddy's questions about finding the length of chain. Her answers couldn't have been particularly enlightening, as she had no real information about the chain beyond Watson leading her to it.

The officer had confirmed that the length of chain was consistent with the blunt-force trauma Charles had suffered.

She shivered at the thought and tapped Watson lightly on the end of his nose. "You'd best stay as innocent as you look today, young man," she said. "We may have to go visit Evelyn again. I know you're not a fan of her kitties, but we need information she might be able to give us. Besides, you need to work on your manners with guest pets."

The only response she got from Watson was a sneeze.

"I hope you're not catching a cold, though it would serve you right for running off so often. Just in case, you'd better ride to the manor in my coat." She scooped him up and was soon out the door, crunching across the icy ground on the way to the manor. She intended to catch Evelyn at breakfast and ask her to drop by the library for a chat. As much as she would have liked to put the whole horrible murder out of her head, she still had to do something to placate Marlene. Somehow she suspected that finding the murder weapon would not be enough.

As it turned out, her timing was perfect. She left Watson at the library and made it to the breakfast room just as Evelyn was coming out. "Hi!" Faith said. "I hope you're still enjoying the retreat in light of everything."

"It's certainly been unusual," Evelyn said. "But then, I get bored easily, so I like unusual. How have you been? I'm certain this isn't exactly how you hoped to spend the days leading up to Christmas."

"Not exactly," Faith said. "But I keep remembering I'll be driving to my mom's house on the day after tomorrow. And I've met some lovely people from the society, so that's good too."

Evelyn raised her eyebrows. "Lovely people? Really? I must have missed them."

"You're definitely one of them. I hope you'll come by the library later. I'd love to sit and chat. Seems I'm always in a rush."

"I'll do that." Evelyn indicated a napkin-wrapped bundle Faith hadn't noticed her carrying. "For now, I'm smuggling a treat up to my babies. They love the sausage here. And later I'm taking them to the pet spa." She laughed lightly. "Imagine, a spa for pets. I certainly have to let the girls experience that. After I drop them off, I'll pop by the library."

"I look forward to it," Faith said. She returned to the library.

Very few society members came by that morning. Apparently she was no longer worth pumping for information. Faith didn't mind, as it gave her time to work on the dozens of little jobs that needed to be done to close up the library for Christmas break.

Nearly an hour passed before Evelyn came into the library. She took a bag from the pocket of her beautiful velvet jacket. "I brought Watson a treat from the spa. You said he liked the fish ones."

"How thoughtful of you. He'll adore you for life." Faith grinned, then motioned to the chairs by the fire. "Let's sit down." She lifted Watson out of one of the chairs and sat.

"It's beautiful here," Evelyn said as she offered Watson a tunaroon. He plucked it delicately from her fingers. "My house is also big and old and beautifully decorated for the holidays." She laughed lightly. "And before you think I'm a terrible egotist, I had nothing to do with the decorating. My husband always hired someone, and now that he's dead, I just keep hiring her." She sighed. "These days it mostly feels empty. I like it here with all the people and drama."

"I could do without the drama," Faith said. "May I ask you something?"

"Yes, but I reserve the right not to answer." She winked.

"Of course. I noticed Mr. Garder and Miss Skimsby . . . gazing at each other yesterday."

"And you want to know if they're dating?" Evelyn said. "I'm really not sure. They are definitely smitten, but they're being very discreet. Which is quite strange for the society. We're normally a rather flamboyant bunch. I can't imagine why they would bother trying to hide the relationship. Neither of them is married."

"I wonder if the relationship had something to do with his black eye," Faith said.

"I don't know the answer to that either," Evelyn said. "Charles gave it to him, but I'm not sure what the fight was about. If I had to guess, I'd imagine Walden didn't like seeing Charles flirt so shamelessly with Caroline. She certainly didn't appreciate the attention."

"No, she didn't seem to." Faith stroked Watson's head distractedly. "Though her mother seemed very fond of Mr. Huffam."

"Only because Octavia is uniquely skilled at creating fantasies for herself and then believing them. Charles's behavior toward women has always been appalling."

"From what I've heard, that wasn't the only behavior of his that was appalling. Have you gotten your jewelry back?"

"Not yet," Evelyn said. "But I'm not really worried about it. I honestly didn't wear those pieces that often outside of Dickens Society events. And once the gala is over, we won't have any other events for months."

"Do you think Mr. Huffam's publishing business was in trouble?" Faith asked. "Maybe that's what made him steal."

"I suppose it's possible. The business was begun by Charles's father. They were old money, and that can run out. It's conceivable that he needed an influx of cash." She handed Watson another treat. "You know what we should do? We should go to the salon. They're playing Victorian parlor games. That might be fun, and no one is using the library. You could come with me."

How sweet. "I'm not sure my boss would go for that. But you should go. It *does* sound fun. What sorts of games?"

"Ones from Dickens's era," Evelyn said. "Charades, blindman's buff, pass the slipper, forfeits."

"I know charades and blindman's buff," Faith said. "But what is pass the slipper? And forfeits?"

Evelyn stood and reached out to tug Faith to her feet. "It's no good to tell you. You should come and play. If your boss tries to scold you, I'll intervene. I promise."

Faith gave in. If Marlene found out she'd deserted her post, she could always tell her she was busy investigating. After all, that was what Marlene had insisted should be her priority. The library was empty, and it might be worthwhile to her assigned investigation to see the society members together.

She followed Evelyn to the salon. Compared with most of the massive rooms in the manor, the salon was positively cozy with wood floors and pale walls. To allow guest activities that required movement, the room was sparsely furnished with two sitting areas, each featuring handsome furniture with silvery-gray upholstery and ornately carved legs.

Faith recognized most of the society members in the room, and she saw that Octavia was still dressed in black, though this dress was simple and modern.

"Are you going to play with us, Miss Newberry?" Walden asked. "I'm delighted. We were just going to start a round of forfeits."

"I don't know what that is."

"I suppose it's a little bit like charades, only much more enjoyable. I'm playing judge. Everyone puts a small item into my top hat after I've gone out into the hall." Walden made a flourish with his top hat to suggest passing it around the room. "When I come back, I pick an object and the person it belongs to must pay a forfeit to get it back."

"What kind of forfeit?" Faith asked.

"A small trick or action," Evelyn explained. "Like whistle a tune or dance. He won't demand anything embarrassing, will you, Walden?"

"Not at all," the tall man said, eyes twinkling.

It still sounded potentially embarrassing, but Faith let Evelyn tow her to one of the love seats in the room.

Walden handed his hat to Caroline and headed for the door.

"No peeking," Caroline called after him.

"How could you even suggest such a thing? I'm offended, madam. Wounded to my very core." He winked and slipped out of the room.

As the hat passed around the room, everyone handed over a small item. Faith wasn't sure what to put in. She searched her pockets and found the small handmade spinning top she'd bought from the vendor for her nephew. She dropped that into the hat.

When Walden came back into the room, he immediately picked out Caroline's earring and insisted she sing a song for everyone. Faith was impressed by the young woman's clear, sweet voice as she sang "Silent Night."

Walden picked a few other items, but Faith was glad that her top wasn't among them. The society members were good sports throughout the game. There was plenty of laughter, but none of it seemed unkind. Marie waltzed around the room with an invisible partner, and Morton whistled "Dixie." As Faith listened to the tune, she was struck with the memory of the book inscription he'd shown her. She still hadn't called Wolfe about it. She made a mental note to follow through with that as soon as possible.

The other members chosen were people she didn't know, but Faith enjoyed seeing them perform various silly antics.

Eventually the time came for the group to move on to the next scheduled event, a recital of Victorian music by various members in the music room.

"Did you enjoy the game?" Evelyn asked Faith as most of the members filed out the door. "I'm sorry you didn't get to do a forfeit."

"I'm not," Faith said sincerely.

Evelyn laughed. "You would have been great. You'll have to excuse me now. I want to run up to check on the girls before the recital. Chat with you later."

As soon as Evelyn hurried out, Faith joined the few left retrieving their items from Walden's hat. She watched the friendly interaction between members, glad to see that not every moment in this group was marked by interpersonal drama.

Finally, Walden and Faith were alone in the salon. She held out her hand. "As you probably guessed, mine is the wooden top."

He dropped it into her hand. "Do you like toys, Miss Newberry?"

"I do, though this one is a gift for my nephew. Oliver likes toys very much."

"I hope he likes that one." Walden looked back into his hat. "Oh, this must be yours as well." He pulled out a single playing card.

"Nope," Faith said. "I only put in the top."

"But it's the last item and you're the last person." He handed her the card. "Are you sure it isn't yours? At any rate, you can have it. I need to dash to the music recital. Caroline is going to play piano."

"She's very talented," Faith said.

"She is," he agreed on his way out the door.

Faith studied the card. It was clearly from the society's special deck. She flipped it over so she could see its face and gasped. The card was the ace of spades and featured the Ghost of Christmas Yet to Come. As in the story, the figure was dressed as Death, in a long, black, hooded cloak, revealing only one skeletal hand.

A hand that pointed directly at Faith.

12

Shaking, Faith slid the card into her pocket. Was the death symbol meant as a message for her, for Walden, or for someone else in the room? Or was it simply an odd coincidence?

With her hand pressed against the ominous card, Faith knew it was time to dig deeper into the backgrounds of the members of the society. Evelyn had been helpful, but some time poking around on the Internet to see if there were any other members she should be watching might be even more helpful. All she needed was a list of the guests, and she knew someone who would be unusually eager to help.

Faith took the back stairs down to the basement. Though wide and well maintained, they lacked the opulence of the gracefully turning staircase that led from the first floor to the second. But then, it would have been mostly for servants when the huge mansion was built, and now it was primarily still for employees of Castleton Manor.

Since the kitchen was housed in the basement, Faith could always count on delicious smells accompanying any visit. She walked by the kitchen entrance and glanced inside, spotting Brooke near the back of the large room, chatting with the head chef. Faith caught her friend's eye and waved quickly before continuing.

The wide basement hallway was lined with doors, each labeled with the name of the office housed behind the door. Faith barely glanced at the signs until she reached the one that read *Assistant Manager*. She took a deep breath and knocked.

"Come in!" Marlene managed to make the invitation sound like an angry demand.

Faith slipped into the room and found Marlene at her desk, flipping through a binder full of papers.

She scowled up at Faith. "I hope you're here to tell me you've found Charles's killer."

"Actually I'm here to get a list of the guests. I want to make sure I'm not overlooking a possible suspect."

"I can't just hand out guest lists to anyone who drops by," Marlene said, slamming the binder closed. "Our guests have an expectation of privacy and it's my job to protect that."

Faith lost her patience. "It's my job to maintain the library, which is the job I prefer to focus on. You're the one who told me to track down the murderer. I would be just as happy to do my real work. Are you telling me to forget about the investigation you demanded?"

"You know I'm not," Marlene snarled.

"Then I need the list," Faith said firmly. "If the murderer isn't you, it must be one of the guests. I need to know all the guests—really know them—if I'm going to figure out which one had a reason to kill Charles."

"Are you any closer to doing that?"

"I'm not sure. What do you know about him?" Faith asked. "Why would the society elect him president when no one seems to like him?"

"I hadn't talked to Charles in years," Marlene said. "And we didn't end on friendly terms, hence the police interest in me. But that also means I don't know much about him and almost nothing personal."

"Do you know if his business was in trouble?" Faith asked. "Could that be why he stole jewelry from other guests?"

"I don't think so. That's one thing I looked into this morning. I asked around among some people I know, and everyone thought

Huffam Publishing was doing well. No one in publishing seems to be getting rich these days, but the company has been around for a couple of generations and has the reputation of being solid."

"Reputations don't always prove to be accurate."

"I'm just repeating what I heard." Marlene turned to her computer and clicked a couple of times. Immediately thereafter, the laser printer near her desk began humming. "I expect you to be discreet with this guest information."

"I will make sure no one else sees it." Faith accepted the sheet of paper. "Do you know if the chief is planning to come by today?"

"Why would he do that?" Marlene snapped.

"I don't know, but I have another playing card to give him." She took the ace of spades from her pocket and held it up. "I received it this morning."

Marlene leaned closer to the card. "That's ominous. Who gave it to you?"

"Walden Garder gave it to me, but I'm not sure if it was from him or if someone was using him to pass along a message." She explained the situation. "It might have been directed at Mr. Garder and not me. Or it might be a coincidence."

"I heard that Walden was angry with Charles," Marlene said. "Maybe he's the killer and someone knows."

"Maybe. Do you know anything about him?"

"Not personally," Marlene said. "He's a stage actor in New York, mostly off-Broadway productions. He doesn't make a lot of money as an actor and lives off a trust fund from his grandfather, I believe."

Faith's eyes widened. "That's quite a bit of information."

Marlene waved a hand. "I chatted with him on the day everyone checked in. He's a surprisingly open person."

Not when I asked him about his fight with Charles. "That's interesting."

"But it's not a motive," Marlene said. "If he'd turned up with the jewelry, I'd have been less surprised. I can't imagine a trust fund will last forever."

"No, probably not." Evelyn had said something similar about old money. Faith tapped the paper. "I'll spend some time with this and see what I can learn."

"Just learn who the killer is," Marlene demanded. "Don't neglect your library duties, but find the killer. Soon."

At least you're not asking for anything difficult, Faith thought as she left the office.

When Faith got back to the library, she was pleased to find Watson innocently settled on her desk. Faith rubbed his ears. "I'm glad one of us is staying out of trouble. I have to do some research." She spotted the book Watson was partially sprawled across. "Oh, right, I have to call Wolfe." She couldn't believe how absentminded she'd been about the book inscription.

She'd just pulled her phone from her blazer pocket when two of the society guests came in. With a small sigh, she put the phone back into her pocket and approached the women with a smile.

One of the women carried a book she'd borrowed from the library collection. "This book was fabulous," she enthused when Faith walked over. "I so appreciate you recommending it. Do you have anything else by this author?"

Like any librarian, Faith felt her heart warm when a book recommendation perfectly meshed with a reader's tastes. She led the woman toward the shelves. "I believe we do have a couple more. And I could make you a list of other authors you might want to try."

"Would you? I'd love that. I'll track them down when I get home." She turned to her friend. "Hazel, didn't I tell you this lady was wonderful?"

"You did," her friend agreed.

After the ladies left, Faith had such a steady stream of guests that she couldn't carve out any time for her research or her phone call to Wolfe. She passed several pleasant hours discussing books and visiting with guests, but she could feel the undone tasks tugging at her. She might have been responding to Marlene's demands when she took on the task of checking out possible suspects in Huffam's murder, but she also truly wanted to know. She had disliked Charles Huffam, but she had found both his body and the murder weapon. She knew she wouldn't be truly free to enjoy Christmas if the question of his murder still weighed on her mind.

Eventually the crowd thinned down as members headed to lunch, and Faith decided to call Wolfe to see when she might bring up the inscribed book to show him. Then if she had time, she'd lunch on a couple of granola bars in her desk and start the search.

But before she could settle down, Walden walked in. "I know you're probably about to close for lunch, but I wanted to return this."

"I don't remember you borrowing a book," Faith said, puzzled.

"I didn't, but Octavia demanded I bring this down for her, as she's 'far too distressed to deal with trivial matters.'" On the last few words, Walden's voice became an amazingly accurate imitation of Octavia's shrill tones.

"She does seem to be very upset about Mr. Huffam's death."

Walden's expression turned sheepish. "You probably think me hard-hearted for mocking her, but I've known Octavia and Charles for years. There was no possible chance that he was going to marry her, despite her imaginary romance."

Faith felt a quiver of excitement that Walden seemed willing to talk now. "Sometimes it's difficult to see the truth when your heart is involved." As she spoke, she was reminded of her last relationship, which had ended badly when she had faced some hard truths.

"I'm not sure how much of Octavia's *heart* was involved," Walden said. "Her pride, certainly, and her hope for a well-heeled husband. But if she'd been realistic, she would have known Charles's interest was in Caroline, not her."

"You couldn't have liked that," Faith said.

The man's face turned guarded. "I don't know what you mean."

"Your interest in Caroline isn't exactly a secret," Faith said. "Nor hers in you. A person doesn't have to be around the two of you for very long to see it. I truly don't understand why you don't make it public."

"I want to go public with it," Walden protested. "But Caroline is certain Octavia wouldn't approve of her being involved with an actor. She's probably right." His shoulders slumped.

"Caroline is an adult."

"I know, but Octavia can be vicious when she's crossed," he said. "Caroline is afraid of her."

"What is she afraid her mother will do?"

He shrugged. "I don't know. She won't tell me, and the one time I pushed, she nearly broke up with me over it. I think Caroline wished her mother would marry Charles, just so she'd have been distracted enough that Caroline might be able to live her own life. Now the old woman has nothing to do but make us miserable."

"I'm so sorry."

Walden seemed to realize he'd just spilled a lot of personal confidences, because he suddenly dropped his gaze. "Look, I have to go. Thank you for being a listening ear. I'd appreciate it if you'd keep what I said to yourself."

Faith uttered something vaguely reassuring, but he fled the library so quickly she wasn't sure if he heard her.

With the library empty, Faith was finally able to call Wolfe.

He answered on the first ring. "Hello, Faith."

He sounded so pleased that at first Faith was speechless. She shook herself and said, "I have a question to ask you about one of the books here. A guest asked me about an inscription, and I don't know anything about it. I was hoping you did."

"Really?" he said. "Why don't you bring it up?"

Again Faith was startled at his willingness to fit her question so easily into his schedule, but she agreed and was soon on her way to the third floor with the copy of *Great Expectations* in her hand.

Wolfe met her in the third-floor vestibule and led her into his living room. As always, Faith admired the stunning view of the ocean from the tall windows that lined the room. The thought of the icy water crashing on the rocks made her shiver.

"Are you cold?" he asked. "I tend to be a little warm-blooded, so I keep the heat turned fairly low up here."

"I'm fine."

Wolfe gestured toward the elegant Victorian sofa. "Why don't you have a seat and tell me about this book?"

Faith obeyed and waited for Wolfe to settle down beside her before handing him the book. "Morton Alried brought it to my attention. He wondered if the inscription could have been written by Martita Hunt. She played Miss Havisham in the movie version of the book in the 1940s."

"I don't know." Wolfe traced the spidery handwriting with a finger. "But I do know that the Wilfred in question is my grandfather Wilfred Jaxon. I was named after him."

Faith smiled, wondering why she didn't know that already. She'd researched the family and the manor before she took the job. "Your name is Wolfe Wilfred?"

He laughed. "No, my first name is Wilfred. Wolfe is a nickname given to me by my grandfather." Again he turned his attention to the book. "Let me call my mother and ask her. She may know for certain about the inscription. I'll let you know what I find out." He stood.

Faith hopped up from the sofa. "Thank you," she said. "I appreciate your looking into it."

"Will you stay for a cup of coffee?" Wolfe asked. "I could have some food brought up as well if you haven't eaten."

At his words, Faith's stomach gave an embarrassing growl, and she felt her cheeks flame.

Wolfe laughed. "It *sounds* as if you haven't eaten."

"The library was really busy this morning," she said. "I was going to have a granola bar at my desk while I did a little work."

Wolfe's eyebrows furrowed. "That's not lunch. You should stay."

Faith didn't know how to turn down the offer without sounding like she was rejecting him, but she doubted Marlene would accept her lunching with Wolfe as a good excuse for not making some progress on figuring out the murderer.

She looked up at her boss's handsome face and suddenly didn't care a bit what Marlene approved. "If I'm not keeping you from something," she said, "I'd love a snack."

Wolfe's expression brightened. "Excellent. I'll make the call, and we'll enjoy the ocean view together for a while."

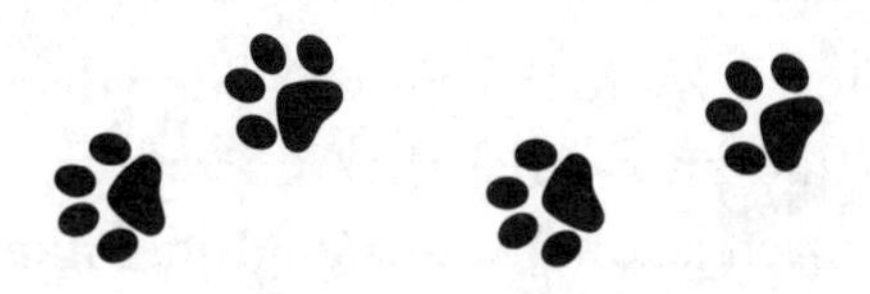

After a delicious lunch and some time talking about sailing—a topic that Wolfe clearly would never grow tired of—Faith had to face a return to work. She opened the library, but since no one was waiting for her attention, she immediately sat down at her computer with the guest list to start her research. She quickly learned that the society was made up of some very influential people including a judge, a college president, and several successful business owners like Charles. Some, like Octavia and Evelyn, were widows of influential people. However, one person seemed not to exist beyond her connections to the society—Marie de Roux.

Faith studied Marie's photo on the society's website. The gaze she turned toward the camera seemed uneasy. The society had short biographies of all the officers, including Marie, the treasurer. Her bio was the shortest of all. It said she was an accountant, but it didn't mention where she worked. Faith could find no other information.

Faith considered herself a private person, but she knew there were half a dozen links that would come up if anyone searched for information about her. Somehow Marie had managed to keep her online information down to a single photo and blurb on the Charles Dickens Society's Web page. Participation in society functions alone had brought up more than that on the other members. Considering how much Marie had obviously disliked Charles, Faith had the strong feeling that this was one mystery woman she needed to learn more about.

13

Faith scooped up Watson and headed out of the library. She'd already taken an extremely long break from it, but since no one seemed interested in books this afternoon, she decided to see if she could get more information on Marie from the one person who always seemed eager to talk about her fellow society members. To her relief, Evelyn was in her room.

"What a lovely surprise," Evelyn said as she opened the door with one of her cats in her arms. "Wasn't that game of forfeits fun? Though I was hoping to hear you sing."

"I love to sing," Faith said, "but I mostly keep it to the shower and church. I'm better as part of a large, large group who are singing very loud."

"Aren't we all?" Evelyn reached out to rub Watson's head. "And my girls will be delighted to get to spend time with their favorite boyfriend."

Faith put Watson on the floor, and Evelyn's cat jumped from her arms to begin washing Watson's face. He backed away until he ran into Faith's leg. Faith stepped around him to follow Evelyn over to sit in one of the two French chairs. "I actually hoped to ask you about Marie de Roux."

Evelyn's eyes lit with interest. "Marie? Do you think she's involved in the burglaries? Or the murder?"

"I don't know," Faith said. "I mostly hoped to learn more about her."

Evelyn deflated and waved her hand. "I don't know her all that well. She's always been pleasant to me, and she's a very good treasurer. We've never had one who did a better job of keeping track of the money and reporting exactly what happens to every penny. You should have seen the last treasurer. The man gave one report annually, and half the time he seemed to be making wild guesses about the money."

"Marie sounds like a definite improvement." Faith startled as Watson raced across the room and leaped onto her lap. She put a calming hand on his back, hoping he wasn't going to get into trouble before she learned more information. "I saw on the society's website that she is an accountant. Do you know what firm she works for?"

"I have no idea. As I said, she's a pleasant person to talk to if you can get her to talk, but she definitely keeps to herself most of the time. I did once have a rousing discussion with her about Dickens's view of stealing as a means of social welfare." She chuckled. "I do know one thing. Marie was never susceptible to Charles's charms. When she first joined the group Charles behaved as he always did with a pretty woman, but Marie slapped him down hard. For a couple of years after that, he acted like she didn't exist. I honestly think that's why she wasn't elected treasurer sooner."

"Charles seemed to have a considerable amount of power in the society," Faith said.

"I know. And that's odd. I certainly never voted for him, and we knocked heads quite often. So did he and Marie once she was elected treasurer. Charles liked to treat the society as his personal kingdom. Marie's insistence on tracking every dime of the society's money definitely cramped his style. And his charm was completely wasted on her. If anything, she liked him less and less as time passed."

"Did he ever go back to flirting with her?" Faith almost winced at the word *flirting*, since *harassing* felt more accurate.

"Not that I saw," Evelyn said. "But something about the man upset her."

Faith's attention was drawn to Watson, who yowled at the two Manx cats on the floor at her feet. Evelyn's cats gazed up at him adoringly, but Faith could feel Watson tensing under her hands. She decided she'd best get him out of here before he ruined her connection with Evelyn by losing his temper with her furry darlings.

"I really should get back to the library." Faith stood, holding Watson close to her chest. "My lunch break was over a long time ago."

"It was lovely seeing you. You know, you ought to come to the ball tomorrow night."

"Ball?" Faith laughed lightly. "I'm sure it would be wonderful, but my wardrobe doesn't lean toward the Victorian. Are you going?"

"I am, mostly because I love watching all the intrigue," Evelyn said. "Though I hope to manage a dance or two. I do enjoy dancing."

"So do I." Faith loved the elegance and flow of ballroom dancing. Perhaps she would come by just to watch. She imagined it would be beautiful.

She was still a little distracted by the thought as she bid Evelyn good afternoon and went out into the hallway.

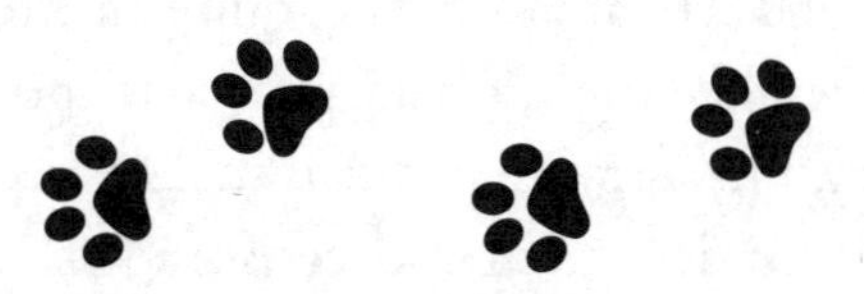

As the suite door closed, the cat cast a scornful eye over his human's arm at the vapid faces of the two ridiculously friendly cats. Good riddance. It had taken his human long enough to realize they needed to leave. He loved his human dearly, but he had to admit she could be slow-witted sometimes. It was a good thing she had him to look after her.

He sniffed the hallway air as his human carried him past doors. He could smell dogs behind some of them, and he sneezed lightly in contempt. Why would humans consider surrounding themselves with those slobbery creatures? Then he caught a new scent. One he recognized.

Not far down the hall, one of the doors was cracked and he smelled bacon on the other side. And liver. Though bacon and liver weren't as good as fish, he was willing to make allowances.

Then his human stopped near the elevator as if she didn't intend to check out the delicious smell at all. The cat could not let that pass. He leaped out of her arms and raced for the suite door.

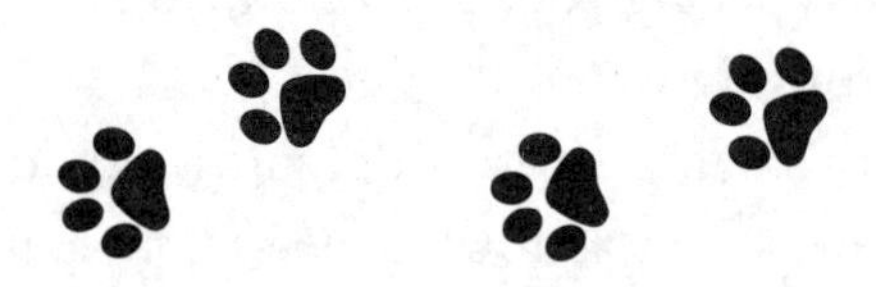

"Watson!" Faith cried as the cat sprinted toward the hall leading to the smaller suites. She rushed after him, calling his name again. If he heard her, he paid no attention.

The door to one of the suites was open a crack, and Watson nudged the crack wide enough to slip in before Faith could catch up. By the flurry of barks she heard on the other side of the door, she knew Watson's arrival was having quite an effect.

When she reached the door, she pushed it open while rapping on it. "I'm sorry. I'm sorry," she said as she entered the room.

The beautifully decorated suite consisted of a sitting area and a comfortable bedroom area, separated by an ornamental screen. Faith didn't have a chance for any more admiration since her attention was drawn to Marie, who was chasing her tiny poodle around the room as the dog chased Watson.

Faith tried to cut Watson off and bent to grab the cat, but he jumped over her reaching hands and used her shoulder as a springboard to the marble top of the antique Edwardian dresser. The cat immediately shoved his head into a paper Happy Tails bag that rested between the two built-in glove boxes on either side of the antique dresser's mirror.

"You naughty boy." Faith scooped up the cat, who gave her an annoyed look as he chewed. She turned to Marie, who had just caught her little poodle. "I'm so sorry. Watson got away from me in the hall. He has a nose like a bloodhound when it comes to the Happy Tails treats they sell down in the spa."

"That's all right," Marie said, giving her dog a hug. "My Bijou can be a handful when she finds something she wants." She chuckled lightly and reached out to pet Watson's head. "Does this dashing fellow have you wrapped around his finger—or paw—as much as my little one has me around hers?"

"He certainly tries. Thank you so much for understanding." Faith's gaze drifted around the room. She didn't want to waste her chance to see where the mystery woman was staying. She noticed a spilled deck of playing cards on the marble top of the coffee table in the sitting area. "Oh, you have a deck of the society cards. I bought one during the vendor fair. They are lovely. Didn't I hear you posed for one of the cards?" Faith asked as she started over to the table.

Marie rushed ahead of her and set the poodle on the fainting couch so she could quickly gather up the cards. "It was a rather silly promotional idea. I wouldn't bother owning a deck, but I've always been fond of solitaire." She shoved the cards into her jacket pocket. "I don't mean to hurry you along, but I have a terrible headache. I was going to rest awhile."

"I'm sorry to hear that. Is there anything I can get you?" Faith asked. "I could go down to the gift shop for some pain reliever if you like."

"No, I'm fine. I just need to rest in the quiet for a little while." As she spoke, Marie herded Faith toward the suite door. "And do not worry about your handsome cat. It was good for *ma chérie* to get a little exercise and excitement. I am a dull mistress."

Before Faith could utter another apology she found herself out in the hallway with the door closed in her face. As she cuddled Watson close, she felt surer than ever that Marie was hiding something. But was it murder?

14

When Faith returned to the library, she plunked Watson down on the floor near her desk. "Try not to get me in trouble for the next few hours, okay, Rumpy?" she said, using the pet name she had given him because of his stub of a tail.

At the mention of his nickname, the cat glared at her, then began grooming away any residue from his adventure.

Since the library was empty, Faith paced in front of the fireplace. Had Marie become so stressed about Faith seeing the deck of cards because certain cards were missing from the deck? And why was there so little information about her online?

Hearing the sound of footsteps, she turned toward the library door with a welcoming smile, which froze on her face when Wolfe came in. For an instant she worried that Marie had complained to him about Watson's trespass into her room. "Wolfe!" she said with a gaiety that rang false to her own ears. "How nice to see you."

He looked at her oddly. "Are you feeling all right?"

"I'm fine. A little jumpy, I guess."

"You seemed all right earlier."

"Watching the ocean is surprisingly relaxing." She noticed the leather-bound book in his hand. "Did you find out about the book inscription?"

"Yes, I called my mother and she remembered it. The signature *was* from Martita Hunt. My grandfather met her when he was out in California for meetings about the possibility of investing in a film. He had this copy of *Great Expectations* with him. It was his favorite book, and he intended to reference it when he talked about the film. Martita Hunt was working on a different film, but she saw the book and they struck up a conversation."

"What a wonderful story," Faith said. "Mr. Alried will be glad to hear it, I'm sure. He asked me to learn if you'd consider selling it, but since it's steeped in family history, I'll assume not."

Wolfe handed the book to her. "No, tell him I'm sorry, but this one will have to stay in the library." He studied her face. "You look a little tired. Are you not sleeping well?" His expression of concern deepened. "I'm so sorry I dragged you to the tree lighting. I feel like it was the beginning of all the unpleasantness you've been subjected to. It certainly didn't turn into the magical experience I'd hoped."

"That's not your fault. I'm sure the tree lighting would have been beautiful. I'll make a point to go next year."

"Good idea. We'll plan on that."

Faith hoped he didn't think she'd been fishing for an invitation a year ahead. Her gaze dropped to the book in her hands. "It was nice of you to come all the way downstairs to tell me about the book. I could have come up to retrieve it."

"My visit is only partly due to the book." The smile that slowly bloomed on his face stayed a bit tentative. "Mostly I was hoping that the other night wouldn't put you off accompanying me to a different event—the Dickens Society ball tomorrow night."

"You don't owe me an invitation to anything," Faith said, completely flustered. She couldn't think of anything worse than to be this man's apology date to a fancy-dress ball.

He raised a hand to stop her protests. "I am not asking because I owe you. In fact, I'd owe *you* for coming with me on such late notice. I originally didn't plan to attend, but in light of the events of this gala, I think I should make an appearance. And I would prefer not to go alone. If you won't come with me, I'll have to ask

Marlene. Please don't make me ask Marlene. I'm sure neither she nor I would enjoy it."

Faith could certainly believe that, but she still shook her head. "I don't see how I can."

"If it will help you decide, don't view it as a date. It will be a retreat function. And you'll be saving a friend from an unpleasant evening."

Faith felt a small nudge of disappointment. "It isn't that. I don't have anything to wear. I know the society members will all be wearing Victorian formal dress. The last time we had a Victorian function, I got away with a hastily gathered ensemble, but a ball is different. If I'm going to be representing the manor with you, I would want to have appropriate clothes." She stopped and pressed her lips together as she recognized that she was babbling.

Wolfe's shoulders relaxed, and his smile grew more confident, warming his eyes. "Oh, is that all? That's easily fixed. For fancy-dress events, the manor often offers rentals to guests who might not have appropriate garb. We partner with a huge costume company out of Boston that brings in the clothes. I'm certain you can still find something suitable. The temporary boutique is next to the gift shop."

"Really?" Faith went to the gift and coffee shop many mornings to grab a coffee, and she had definitely been there since the Dickens Society retreat had begun. She hadn't noticed that the storeroom next door had turned into a costume shop. Apparently her morning coffee really did bring her back to life. "I feel a little silly for not knowing about it," she confessed.

"That's all right. It's easy to miss if you don't know. There won't be any rental fee for you, though. You'll be representing the manor, so we'll pick up the tab."

"You don't have to do that," Faith said, feeling heat rise into her cheeks. She gave herself a little mental shake. *Stop getting silly notions. Wolfe Jaxon and I are employer and employee and maybe friendly acquaintances—that's all we're ever going to be. That's all we ever should be.*

"It's only fair, since you didn't plan to go otherwise," Wolfe said. Before she could respond, he insisted, "It's no trouble, and I won't hear anything else about it. I'll let Iris know to expect you so she'll keep the boutique open a little later this evening. I'll try to make the actual event as painless as possible. It should be quite impressive, given the arrangements we've been making for it. I understand the society members really go all out."

That afternoon, she closed up the library a little early, though it went against her work ethic. The ball was just a work function, she reminded herself, but still she hoped the boutique would have something pretty.

As she walked down the long gallery with Watson in her arms, she saw a group of police officers enter from the other end and head up the curving stairs to the second floor. *Has someone else been robbed? Or worse?*

Though she knew she shouldn't, Faith followed the officers up the grand staircase. As she climbed, she realized she knew all three of them. Bryan Laddy was no surprise, as he'd handled the burglaries so far, but she also spotted Jan Rooney's short black hair and Mick Tobin's stocky build. With three officers paying a visit to Castleton Manor, Faith had the uncomfortable feeling that something bigger than another burglary had happened.

She felt a stab of panic. Surely there hadn't been another murder . . .

Faith expected the officers to stop at Marie's suite, but instead they walked right by it. When they stopped and knocked on a door, Walden answered.

"Mr. Walden Garder," Officer Laddy said, his voice cool and firm, "we need you to come with us to answer some questions about the murder of Charles Huffam."

"I don't understand," Walden said. His face froze. "You couldn't possibly think I killed Charles."

"We have a witness," Officer Tobin piped up. Officer Laddy frowned in his direction, but that didn't stop Tobin from adding, "You were seen fleeing the scene of the murder. The witness recognized your coat. And we've determined the murder weapon was a chain that had been in your possession."

"That's preposterous!" Walden sputtered. "I couldn't have killed Charles. I wasn't even at the tree lighting. I'd planned to go, but I couldn't find my coat."

"You can explain it to the detective at the station," Officer Laddy said as he escorted Walden into the hall.

Faith watched them in shock. She'd made the connection of the chain to the dramatic reading right away, and she'd even seen Charles and Walden fighting in the garden. But though it made sense in her head, she still couldn't quite reconcile Walden with murder.

"Miss Newberry!" Walden peered into Faith's face as he passed her. "Please tell Caroline that it wasn't me. I wouldn't do this. I wouldn't kill anyone!"

"I'll tell her."

As Faith helplessly watched Officers Laddy and Rooney walk the man down the hall, she was startled when Officer Tobin stopped beside her.

"Don't get the lady's hopes up," he warned Faith. "We have a witness description, and we're pretty sure we'll get a match to the DNA on the chain that was used to bash Mr. Huffam in the head."

"I don't remember seeing Walden in any of the carriages that took guests from here to town for the tree lighting," Faith said.

"It wouldn't matter," Tobin said. "He has a car here. He could have taken that."

"But he said he didn't go at all and couldn't find his coat. Maybe it was stolen. The same person could have stolen the chain."

"Could have but didn't. We got the guy, Miss Newberry. You can rest assured." Officer Tobin turned and trotted off down the hall to catch up with the others.

Faith watched them go, wishing she felt nearly as sure as the police officer. Somehow the murder didn't feel solved to her. Not by a long shot.

15

Faith pulled out her phone and called Marlene Russell.

"What?" the other woman screeched into the phone.

"I assume you know about the police taking Walden Garder."

"Yes. I'm down in the main hall now, and I don't have time to talk."

Before Marlene could hang up on her, Faith said, "Tell me again which suite Caroline Skimsby is in."

"Agatha Christie," Marlene snapped before the call ended.

"Thanks," Faith grumbled as she shoved her phone back into her blazer pocket and hurried down the hall toward the Agatha Christie Suite. She knocked on the door and waited, trying not to fidget from nerves and impatience.

No one came to the door.

Faith knocked again, more firmly, in case Caroline or her mother simply had not heard her.

Still no answer.

Faith took out her phone and checked the time, suppressing a yelp as she realized the boutique would be closing soon. *I'll come back up and try to get in touch with Caroline after I get my dress.*

When she reached the first floor, she walked down the corridor leading to the breakfast room, then turned down a narrower passage. She was pleasantly surprised to see Brooke in the gift shop when she walked in.

"Fancy meeting you here," Brooke said cheerfully. "You Christmas shopping too? My mom specifically asked for one of the local artist drawings of the manor. She's awfully proud of my working here."

"As she should be," Faith said. "Actually I'm here to get a dress for the ball."

"The ball?" Brooke echoed. "I didn't know you were going. I'll be helping with some appetizers. No dancing for me."

"I'm sorry to hear that, Cinderella," Faith teased. "My going is kind of a last-minute thing. Wolfe came by and asked if I would attend with him. He wasn't planning to go, but with all the trouble with the robberies and the murder, he felt he had to make an appearance."

"Yeah, this isn't quite what Christmas here is normally like," Brooke said seriously. Then her face brightened. "And I'm clearly not Cinderella. You're the one going to the ball with the prince."

"I'm just going as a work-related activity. Wolfe said so himself."

"Right. I wouldn't mind going to a ball on the arm of one of the most handsome men in Lighthouse Bay. Possibly *the* most handsome. Somehow my work-related activities all involve hot food, not hot guys."

"If you're done," Faith said, rolling her eyes, "can you help me choose a dress? Even though it's work, I want to look nice. Maybe even more so because it's for work."

"I can't imagine you looking bad, but I'll be glad to help. The costumes are all in the storeroom. You can get to them from there." Brooke pointed to a neatly printed sign on the wall not far from the register that had a filigree-style arrow and the words *Gala Gown Boutique*.

Faith couldn't believe she hadn't noticed it when she was in the shop before. *Some detective I am.*

She followed Brooke into the large storeroom that had been cleared, leaving only some built-in shelves along one wall. The shelves were currently covered with stacks of shoe boxes. In the middle of the room, a long rack held gowns.

Iris stood next to the rack, pushing aside some dresses, stopping at a dark-red velvet gown. "Faith, I'm sorry I didn't hear you come into the gift shop. I snuck back here to straighten up after Wolfe called to say you'd be down to find a dress. I figured since Brooke was browsing, she could yell for me if someone popped in."

"That's perfectly fine. Brooke helped me find my way."

"It's not that obvious," Iris said. "The guests know because there's a flyer specifically about it in the welcome packet they received when they checked in for the gala." She tilted her head. "Do you have any idea what color gown you want? You could pull off red with your chestnut hair."

"I hadn't really thought about it," Faith said, though she didn't like the idea of anything quite as bold as the red velvet dress Iris indicated. She told the woman her size. "Can I just see what you have that might fit?"

"Absolutely." Iris began pulling gowns off the rack. She hung five along the edge of the built-in shelves so Faith could look at them.

Faith quickly eliminated one gown in drab shades of brown and a pink one with so many ribbons and ruffles that it reminded her of a birthday cake.

"This one is pretty," Faith said as she touched the skirt of a simple gray dress with minimal black lace trim.

"That's too plain," Brooke insisted. "You don't have to disappear into the background." She gestured to a gown in burgundy taffeta with a wide pleated ruffle along the bottom, an overskirt in the same shade of burgundy, and a tightly fitted black bodice that dipped alarmingly low. "That one would grab some attention."

"I'm not sure that neckline is quite my style. I want to breathe and feel completely clothed at the same time." Faith studied the fifth dress. It was black velvet and heavily embroidered in burgundy silk. The neckline was very high, but the black reminded her too much of the mourning clothes that Octavia had been wearing. Faith sighed. "Maybe the brown one would be all right after all." It would be better to come across as a dead leaf than a mourner.

"I do have one other," Iris said. "I didn't bring it out because the hem was badly torn when one of our guests tried it on. But if you like it, I should be able to repair the gown in time for you to wear."

"Can I see it?"

Iris walked to the far end of the clothes rack and came back carrying a gown of silvery blue. The bodice was fitted and would have been every bit as low as the burgundy gown except for a lace upper bodice and narrow stand-up collar in the same shade of blue. Though there was a pleated trim at the bottom and on the shoulders, the dress didn't feel fussy.

"That's so pretty. What do you think?" Faith asked Brooke.

"I think you should try it on."

Iris and Brooke helped Faith into the dress so that she didn't accidentally tear the hem further. The cut of the dress made Faith's waist look tiny, and the skirt swished as she walked. She felt like a princess in a fairy tale.

"That one," Brooke said. "Get that one." She glanced up at a clock on the storeroom wall and gasped. "And since that decision is made, I have to run. I'm late for the dinner rush. I've got someone covering for me, but the chef is going to flip out if I don't get down there right now."

"Are you going to get in trouble because of me?" Faith asked anxiously.

Brooke waved it off. "I'll tell her I was helping Wolfe Jaxon's date pick a dress. All will be forgiven. See you later." With that, she dashed out.

Iris chuckled. "She is always a breath of fresh air. Let me help you out of that dress."

"Are you sure it won't be a problem to repair the hem?" Now that she had it on, Faith could see that part of the box-pleated ruffle at the bottom of the dress hung loose.

Iris patted her arm. "Don't fret. I'll repair it and press it and have someone deliver it to the cottage. The dress will be there by the time you need it. Do you want to look at shoes? We have a great selection."

"I think I'm okay on shoes," Faith said. "I have heels that should work. Not that anyone will see them."

Faith took one last peek at herself in the mirror before slipping out of the dress, surprised by her reluctance to shed her finery. She walked out to the main part of the gift shop with Iris. "I really love that gown. You're a lifesaver."

"I'm happy to help," Iris said. "The dress is lovely on you. I'm with Brooke on this. Wolfe may be quite smitten when he sees you."

"It's a work function."

"Whatever you say, dear." Iris chuckled and headed behind the counter.

Caroline stuck her head in the door of the gift shop. When her gaze locked on Faith, she marched in. "Are you the one who made the police come after Walden?" she demanded.

"I'm not in control of the police department. I couldn't make them come after someone if I wanted to," Faith said, immediately put on the defensive. "And I certainly had no desire to see Walden arrested or even questioned. I did see him leave with the police, though. He said to tell you that he's innocent."

Caroline huffed in exasperation. "Of course he's innocent. It's absurd to even think otherwise. Walden is the kindest, dearest man." Tears filled the young woman's eyes, and she put her hands over her face.

"Please don't worry too much," Faith said, regretting her harsh tone. "The police in Lighthouse Bay are very good. If there's been a misunderstanding, they'll figure it out."

Caroline dropped her hands and her damp eyes blazed. "There's no 'if' about it. Walden didn't kill anyone, not even that odious Charles Huffam."

"Apparently someone saw a person near the tree where Mr. Huffam's body was found. The person was wearing Mr. Garder's coat. And the length of chain used in the dramatic reading may have been the murder weapon. Do you have any idea how someone could have gotten ahold of those things?"

"The chain didn't belong to Walden," Caroline said. "I think he got it from Charles. Knowing Charles, I'm sure he wanted it back the second the reading was over for the night. As for the coat, Walden has always been casual with his things. He could simply have left it hanging on a chair or a coatrack."

Faith mentally filed that information away. Then she had a different thought. "What can you tell me about Marie de Roux?"

Caroline perked up. "Why? Do you think Marie is the killer? Are the police questioning her too?"

"I don't know the extent of the police investigation, and I have no idea who killed Mr. Huffam, but I'd like to know more about Miss de Roux. She seems very mysterious."

"She is really private," Caroline admitted. "Though I've always found her nice enough. She certainly loves that little dog. She and Evelyn got into a row once because Evelyn wanted to bring her cats to a society meeting and didn't want any dogs there. Apparently her cats have a *phobia*." She rolled her eyes.

"How did they resolve it?"

"I think Marie gave in," Caroline said. "She's not one to draw a lot of attention to herself. But then Walden brought his dog to the meeting, which he normally never did. I think he hated the unfairness of Evelyn's bullying Marie." She sniffled. "Walden hates to see anyone treated badly."

"How did Miss de Roux and Mr. Huffam get along?" Faith asked.

"She didn't like him. And he hated her. I overheard a fight between Marie and Charles on the opening day of this gala. I was flabbergasted because Marie isn't one to stand her ground. Anyway, I didn't get any particulars. They stopped talking as soon as they realized I was there. But Charles wanted Marie to do something, and he threatened to offer everyone a peek at her skeleton if she refused."

"Her skeleton?"

Caroline shrugged. "I thought it was a euphemism for something crude. Charles was a crude guy for all that he tried to cover his crudity with Dickens quotes."

"Maybe he meant that she had a skeleton in her closet."

"Could be. I didn't hear more than that."

Faith chatted with Caroline for a bit longer until the young woman seemed calmer and less inclined to cry. It was clear Caroline was cheered by the idea that there might be someone else suspicious for the police to consider. "Are you going to tell the police about Marie?"

"The police will find the real killer," Faith said. "Trust them."

"That would be easier if they let Walden go."

When Faith left the gift shop, she was relieved to head for home, where a nice quiet evening by the fire awaited. She would even try not to worry about the ball or ponder what the likelihood was of her tripping on the full skirt of her elegant gown and falling on the floor in front of Wolfe.

She collected Watson and set off down the dark path for the cottage. With the long nights of winter, she wondered if she should start driving to the manor and parking in the staff lot. On the other hand, that parking lot was still a bit of a hike to the house, just from a different direction. Faith wasn't sure she'd be saving much time, and when the winter snows really arrived, she might be glad for the ability to walk from the cottage to the main house.

Faith could hear the sound of the surf breaking at the beach not far from the house. She'd enjoyed walking on the little beach when she'd first arrived, but the icy winds blowing off the water made it unlikely she'd be taking beach walks anytime soon. Just the thought made her shiver inside her thick coat. If she were to see the beach in the next few months, it would be through a window at the manor. That thought brought back the memory of sitting on the sofa with Wolfe and gazing out at the waves, and she indulged in the memory for a while.

Trotting along beside her, Watson must have grown impatient with his dreamy mistress. He ran ahead, then cast an impatient look back at Faith and meowed.

"I'm coming," she muttered. "I know you're hungry, but you won't get fed faster if I slip and fall."

Watson meowed again and ran on, disappearing into the shadows ahead.

"Don't get lost!" Faith yelled after him. "I am not going to spend hours out here trying to find you." She hoped her bluff convinced him, but she doubted it. He knew as well as she did that she would never leave him out in the cold. Unfortunately, that chance seemed more and more likely as she followed the twists and turns of the garden paths and saw no sign of her stumpy-tailed cat.

When she left the garden behind and walked the last steps to the cottage, she spotted Watson sitting right by the front door, staring up at it.

"You can stare at the door all you want, but you won't make it open before I get there," Faith said. "That's the beauty of opposable thumbs."

Strangely, Watson didn't turn toward her. He might not always obey her, but the cat could usually be counted on to at least look when she spoke to him.

"What is so exciting about the door?"

When she got close enough to see for herself, she froze. Another ace of spades was pinned to the front door with a stiletto dagger . . . which dripped red.

16

After Officer Mick Tobin finished taking a series of photos of the playing card, he braced one gloved hand against the door for leverage and grabbed the stiletto with the other. "Do you have any idea why someone would be sending you threatening messages, Miss Newberry?" he asked as he jerked the blade free of the door. He caught the card before it could flutter to the ground.

"No," Faith said softly, "but I think this is the second warning I've gotten."

With the gruesome stiletto still clutched in his hand, the officer turned to her, one eyebrow raised. "The second?"

Faith explained about the playing card left in Walden's hat during the game of forfeits. "As ominous as it was, I couldn't be sure that it wasn't just a coincidence."

"It doesn't seem to be in light of this." The officer sniffed the blade. "If it makes you feel any better, this isn't blood. It's ketchup. Could this be someone's idea of a joke?"

"My friends don't have that kind of sense of humor," Faith said with a shudder. *For which I am grateful.*

Officer Tobin held the blade closer to the light shining down from the fixture next to the door. He examined the stiletto. "The blade is pretty dull, though the tip is sharp. I think maybe this is a letter opener that's designed to resemble a knife. The handle is pretty fancy."

"I wonder if it might have come from one of the vendor carts this week," Faith said. "I know there was a vendor selling that specific playing card design, but I don't remember seeing a letter opener like that."

"We'll check it out." He opened an evidence bag and dropped the blade into it. "So the first ace of spades was given to you by Mr. Garder."

"Yes, but he seemed to think it was mine. There were a number of society members playing the game. Any of them could have put the card into the hat. For all I know, the warning was intended for Walden and not me."

"This one is certainly aimed at you."

Faith caught sight of the sticky blade in the bag, and a chilling thought came to her. "Maybe the killer is warning both of us."

"Maybe, but only one of you is a suspect in the murder of Mr. Huffam. You're not the one we hauled to the police station this afternoon."

"As you pointed out, Walden was taken down to the police station this afternoon. So he couldn't have left this."

"When were you last here at the cottage?" Tobin asked.

"This morning."

"So Mr. Garder could have left the card before he was taken."

"Do you think the ketchup was on the blade that long?"

Tobin shrugged. "It didn't look exactly fresh, but I don't know how fast ketchup dries. One of our lab guys will probably be able to figure it out."

Faith twisted her hands together. She thought of Caroline's certainty that Walden couldn't possibly be the killer and her own questions about Marie. "Actually I saw that same deck of cards today in the room of one of the guests," Faith said. "Marie de Roux. The cards were spilled out on a table, and she became very antsy when I said something about them. She snatched them up right away. She could have wanted to be sure I didn't notice the missing ace and maybe some other missing cards as well."

"Ms. de Roux?" Tobin echoed. "She's the society secretary, right?"

"She's the treasurer. Are you looking into her as well?"

He gave her a stern look. "Even if I knew, I couldn't tell you. You know that. But I'm not the lead investigator on the case by a long shot. I just saw a Dickens Society member list this afternoon, and I've got a good memory. So you think we should investigate her because she cleaned up spilled playing cards?"

Faith folded her arms. "There's no reason to try to make me sound stupid."

Officer Tobin held up his hands. "No ma'am. I was just wondering if you had any further insights to share with me."

Faith wasn't sure, but she suspected he might not be taking her seriously. Still, his expression stayed innocent and curious. "Well, on the night of the first burglary, I didn't see Marie until late in the reading, and she wasn't dressed like the rest of the society members."

He cocked an eyebrow. "She wasn't?"

"No, most of the members were wearing these elaborate Victorian costumes, but Marie wore regular modern clothes."

"And she was the only member not dressed up?" Tobin asked.

Faith thought back to the crowd that night. "Not the *only* member, no. But one of the few, definitely. And she didn't like Charles Huffam."

"It seems there was a lot of dislike for Mr. Huffam going around," Tobin said. "Not to be disrespectful, but the fact that she was one of a few people who didn't want to wear a costume doesn't exactly make her suspicious. Maybe she's just sensible. Some people don't like to dress up, especially in outlandish getups like that."

"There's something else. Caroline Skimsby overheard an argument between Marie and Charles. Apparently he wanted her to do something, and she was resisting. In the argument, he threatened her about revealing a skeleton."

"Miss Skimsby told you about this argument, but you didn't personally overhear it." His tone did not convey that he was impressed.

Faith knew where this was going, but she wasn't ready to give up. "Caroline told me about it this afternoon."

"After her boyfriend was picked up. Did it occur to you that she might have been using you to distract us?"

"How did you know he was her boyfriend? Their relationship was supposed to be a secret."

"I was in the hall when Mr. Garder begged you to tell Miss Skimsby that he wasn't guilty, remember?" the officer said. "I can spot a man in love easily enough. And that means Miss Skimsby is likely to say anything to divert attention."

"I understand that, but I still feel that Marie is important to everything that's happened." Faith was beginning to feel helpless. She wasn't making any headway with this conversation. But how could she? She had no real evidence, only a hunch that something was off about the woman.

"I will be sure to pass your concerns about Ms. de Roux on to the chief, but I can't promise he'll put much stock in it without any proof. We can't build a case without evidence."

Frustrated, Faith knew there wasn't much more she could expect.

Officer Tobin checked the inside of the cottage, and then Faith was able to go in.

Watson rushed over and began meowing frantically.

"I know," she told him. "Sorry for shoving you inside earlier. I'll fix supper now. I'm hungry too."

She knew the cat's concern for her hunger was probably limited, so she went ahead and fed him first so he'd stay out from under her feet. She gave up on her plan to fix herself something nice and microwaved some leftover chicken and vegetables. It wasn't one of her fancier meals, but she'd reached a point where she didn't care.

Faith had just finished eating and putting the dishes in the sink when the phone rang. She hurried over to the front door where she'd hung her coat and blazer on hooks and fished her phone out of her pocket. Her mother's number flashed on the screen.

Faith answered as she headed for the chair by the fire. "Hi, Mom, how are you?"

"I'm fine but how are you? You're still going to be home for Christmas, aren't you?"

"That's the plan and it's been the plan all along. We have one more day of this Charles Dickens Society event, then the ball tomorrow night. The day after tomorrow I'll close up the library and head home. I'll most likely get there late."

"I saw on the news there was another murder in Lighthouse Bay," her mother said. "Please tell me you're not getting involved with that."

Faith sighed. "I can't tell you that. I *am* involved, at least peripherally. The victim was a guest here—the society president. And I was at the tree lighting when the body was found." She decided it would be better for her mother's nerves to withhold the fact that Faith was the one to find the body, with Watson's help.

"Does your aunt know about this?" her mother demanded.

Faith knew sometimes her mother could be a little competitive with Aunt Eileen, especially since Faith had taken the Castleton Manor librarian position and saw Eileen far more often. She picked her next words carefully. "Well, everyone in Lighthouse

Bay knows about the murder. But the police picked up a suspect today, so I'm sure they're going to solve the case anytime now." She tried to think of the last part of her statement as hope instead of the lying that it felt more like.

"You need to stay out of it," her mother said. "You're a librarian, not a detective, and you seem to end up in the middle of these things far too much."

"I'll do my best but it's hard. I'm not the one pulling me into it." Faith gave in and told her mom about the things that had occurred so far. "So Marlene and Brooke and Caroline are all begging me to poke around for their own reasons. Plus, these cards are some kind of message directed at me by someone. With all that, I don't know how to stay completely out of the situation."

"Well, I do," her mother said. "The answer is simple. Come home right now. Just take the last day as a sick day or something and come home."

"A sick day?" Faith echoed. "You want me to lie to my employer and say I'm sick when I'm perfectly healthy? You want me to shirk my responsibilities?"

"I want you to be safe and come home." Her mother's voice softened. "I won't stop worrying until you're home. Even without this horrible murder. After all, this is New England, and a blizzard could be along any day to keep you from getting home safely for Christmas."

"There are no blizzards in the weather forecast, Mom. It'll be fine."

Her mother snorted softly. "Like New England weather forecasters ever get it right. I've always maintained they come up with their forecasts by throwing runes."

"I'm pretty sure there aren't going to be any blizzards. I'll be home the day after tomorrow, but it'll be after dark since I have to close up the library before I can leave. Still, I'll be there before bedtime."

"Just be careful, darling," her mother insisted. "You're a woman all alone. And you're far too brave for your own good sometimes."

"I'm not all alone," Faith reminded her. "I have friends and Aunt Eileen in Lighthouse Bay. Honestly, I'm almost never really alone."

"I just mean that you're without a man and a family of your own. Now that's something you should be doing with your spare time, meeting a nice man. Eileen says your boss seems nice. And handsome."

Oh, now *you're in favor of what Aunt Eileen says*. "He's very nice and he's my boss. There is no better way to ruin a good job than to be involved with the boss. I seem to remember you telling me that years ago."

"That was before you reached nearly forty without getting married."

Thanks for making me feel old, Mom. There was no way Faith was going to tell her mother that Wolfe was going to be her date of sorts for the ball. "I'm only a two-hour drive from Springfield. I have a job to do, and I'm going to do it, but I'll be home as I planned. Try not to worry."

"Someday when you have children of your own we can talk about how much mothers worry. But you stay out of trouble."

"I will." She was just about to end the call when her mother latched on to something she'd said earlier.

"Didn't I hear you say there was a ball tomorrow night? Do you mean a fancy ball with dancing?"

"Yes. Exactly that kind of ball."

"Are you going?"

"I am," Faith said with a mental sigh, "because it is a work event."

"But you will be wearing a gown?"

"Yes, I will be wearing a gown." She knew where this was going.

"You should come home tomorrow. You don't need to go to a ball. Are you going with a date?"

"Like I said, it's a work event," Faith said. "Now I really need to clean up the kitchen so I can get to bed. It's been a long day. You have a good night. I love you."

Faith had to give her mom several more "good nights" and "I love yous" before she got off the phone. She ended with more reassurances that she would stay out of trouble and be home as planned. As she dropped the phone back into her pocket, she hoped she could live up to the promises she'd just made.

17

Ice-coated snow crunched under Faith's bare feet as she stumbled through the huge hedge maze, sometimes colliding with the sharp branches in the darkness. Behind her, someone laughed, a high-pitched cackle of demented glee. Faith turned, squinting into the blackness, but the figure never came close enough to be identifiable as more than a lurching, hulking shadow. She ducked as an ace of spades whistled through the air, zipping by her like a ninja throwing star from the movies.

"Leave me alone!" she yelled, her words snatched away by the bitter wind and spread as thin as a whisper. "What do you want?"

Another card whistled through the air and embedded itself in the end of Faith's nose. It hurt. It really hurt.

"Ow!" She sprung up in bed, knocking Watson from his position on her chest, and rubbed her nose. It still hurt a little. "Did you bite my nose, you little monster?"

Watson looked at her innocently, then gave an impatient meow, raced to the end of the bed, and leaped off.

Faith got out of bed, shoved her feet into her slippers, and grabbed her robe. "Wanting breakfast is no excuse for attacking me."

She'd shuffled out of the bedroom before she realized she could hear someone knocking on the door to the cottage.

Watson stared at her from a few feet away.

"Were you trying to tell me someone was here?" she asked, pulling her bathrobe closer.

He turned and padded off, a smug expression on his furry face.

Faith hurried to the front door and opened it.

A young woman with a pink nose and cheeks stood bundled up against the cold with a garment bag in her arms. She sniffled, then thrust the bag toward Faith. "Mrs. Alden told me to bring this over." Her voice was thick, as though her nose was stopped up.

"Yes, thank you." Faith let the young woman pile the heavy garment bag into her arms. "Do you want to come in and warm up?"

"I better not. After I deliver this, I have to run a bunch of errands for Ms. Russell. She's not very patient, and I had to wait here for a while."

"Sorry," Faith said. "I was asleep. Why didn't you ring the bell?"

The young woman sniffled again. "I did. You must have been sleeping hard. Anyway, there you go. Merry Christmas." At that she spun around and started walking away. Almost immediately she spun back around. "Did you know you have a hole in the door and something red and sticky smeared on it?"

Faith sighed. "It's ketchup." At the woman's puzzled glance, she added, "It's a long story."

The young woman didn't comment. She just nodded, then wished Faith another merry Christmas and headed back toward the manor.

"Merry Christmas," Faith called out after her and then closed the door.

The gown was heavy in her arms, reminding Faith that she'd never worn anything like it. At least it would probably be warm with so much fabric. She carried it back to her bedroom.

Faith decided to leave the gown in the bag where it would be safe from Watson's claws or teeth, and she headed off to the kitchen to make breakfast. "I appreciate the wake-up call," she told him as she filled his bowl. "But be gentle next time. I don't need teeth marks in the end of my nose."

She'd barely settled down at the table with her coffee when the phone rang. She was glad to see it wasn't her mom again, though she'd half-expected it.

Instead, Aunt Eileen launched right in and announced, "Before I say anything else, let me preface it with this: your mother made me call."

"Mom is a little worked up," Faith said, wondering how it was possible that she was completely exasperated within ten minutes of waking. "She always gets crazy at Christmastime. I think she gets this huge 'perfect Christmas' thing stuck in her head and then freaks out whenever anyone deviates from the program. I don't know what has made her think I'm going to miss it this year."

"It couldn't be because someone is sending you creepy messages," Eileen said. "And why did I have to hear about that from Barbara? I'm right here."

"It only happened yesterday," Faith protested. "And the police don't think it's anything to worry about. It *was* creepy, but at least the stuff on the letter opener was only ketchup."

"Even so, your mother and I both think you should take this seriously," Eileen said impatiently. "Are you still planning to leave for Springfield tomorrow? I was going to stay here another day and ride out with Eric and Claire and the kids, but I could get someone to cover for me at the library and leave with you tomorrow. I know your mother would like it better if you weren't driving alone."

"As I told Mom, it's only two hours," Faith said. "I've driven a lot farther alone and in worse weather. And I know you want to spend the travel time with your grandkids. Mom is being a tiny bit irrational."

Eileen sighed. "Okay, I'm not supposed to tell you this, but she had a dream."

"A dream?"

"I know it's silly. Barbara knows it's silly too, but bear with me. Barbara said she had a dream about a woman lying on the floor in a fancy dress and surrounded by blood. And when you told her you were going to a ball, she's now convinced the woman was you. So I'm supposed to talk you into skipping the ball and going home today."

Faith found the coincidence a little chilling, but she certainly wasn't going to walk out on a work commitment for a dream. If she could ignore her own dream about playing cards flying around, then she could ignore her mother's dream as well. Especially since Iris had gone to the trouble of repairing the beautiful ball gown so Faith could wear it.

"I can't leave early. Today is the day the guests will be returning any books they borrowed. Besides, I need to close up the library before I leave, and I can't do that while there's an ongoing event. I understand that the dream scared Mom, and I can even see why, but the most I can do is promise to be careful, just like I told Mom last night."

"See that you do," Eileen said. "And if your mom calls, tell her I tried to get you to leave early, but you were too stubborn. Otherwise I have a feeling she'll show up on my doorstep."

"No way. I'm going to tell her that you suggested I stick around until the following day to avoid driving the winter roads at night," Faith teased.

"If you do that, I'll come after you myself, and people have always said I'm the more frightening sister. Either way, you're in trouble. And now that we've covered your impending demise, I have a problem."

"What's that?"

"I drew your dad's name for the Christmas Eve gift exchange. You know he's the toughest one in the whole family to buy for.

Martin never wants anything, at least that he mentions. I've gone through every shop in Lighthouse Bay, and nothing jumps out at me. What do you suggest?"

"You're buying him something?" Faith said as concern swept through her. "We drew names months ago. You always knit your Christmas Eve gift. Are your hands bothering you more than usual?"

"No. I mean, yes, they ache something fierce this time of year, but no more than any other year. I knitted Martin a sweater with a fish on it."

"That sounds perfect. Dad loves to fish."

"Yes, but the fish came out so goofy. I don't know what's wrong. It looked okay in the pattern, but the finished version is definitely smirking. Not even blocking helped, and blocking fixes everything. My tension must have been off, but I've knitted tons of colorwork and never had this problem before." Faith could practically see her aunt wringing her hands over the misshapen fish.

"I think you should give it to him," Faith said. "You know his sense of humor. Dad would love a smirking fish sweater. He'll wear it everywhere."

"Are you sure? Maybe you could come by and approve it before I wrap it up."

"Sure, I'll be glad to." She heard knocking. "Hold on. Someone is at the door."

Faith crossed the room, stumbling along the way as Watson dashed under her feet. "Watson, cut it out." She tripped again and stopped to finish the call. "I don't know if I can get there today with everything, but if not, I'll call, and we'll get together tomorrow before I leave. I have to go answer the door, and I need to hang up since Watson seems to be trying to kill me along the way."

"None of that," Eileen ordered. "No broken legs before Christmas."

"Tell that to Watson." As soon as Faith ended the call, whoever was on the other side of the door pounded harder.

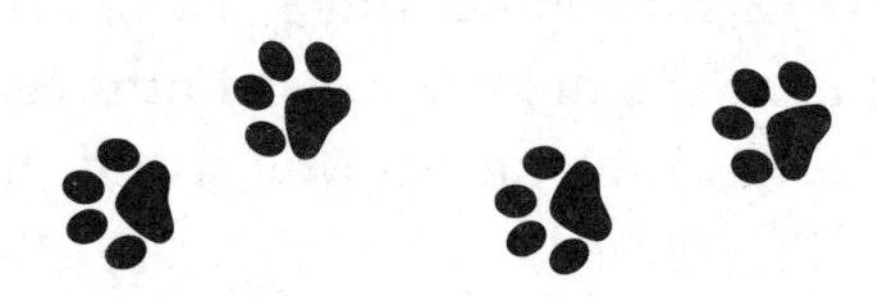

The cat couldn't believe his human wasn't paying attention to him so he slipped between her feet.

She reprimanded him again. "Rumpy! Knock it off."

As much as he loathed the ridiculous and undignified nickname, he simply couldn't let his human answer that door. Couldn't she hear the anger in the pounding fist? Couldn't she smell the stench of dog wafting under the tiny crack at the bottom of the door? How could she not recognize that smell?

His human wasn't picking up his message from his interference with her ankles, so he grabbed the back of her pajama pants and pulled, accidentally grazing her skin in the process and making her cry out. Certainly she'd realize he was only protecting her.

Instead his human scooped him up and carried him back to the bedroom. She tossed him in a very undignified way on top of the garment bag on the bed. He raced her to the door, but she used a foot to push him to one side and closed the door in his face.

He heard her footsteps heading away from him. He yowled in distress as he realized he had no way to get there and keep her safe.

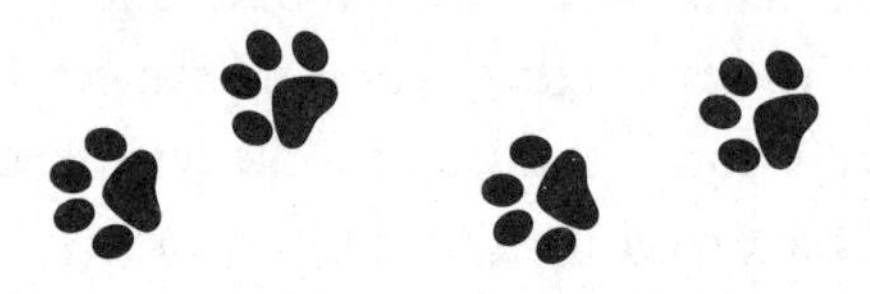

With Watson safely closed up in the bedroom, Faith hurried toward the front door, singing out, "I'm coming!" Still annoyed by the difficulty with Watson, she flung open the door and gaped.

Marie stood there with her little poodle in her arms and a murderous expression on her face. Faith started to swing the door closed, but the other woman blocked it with one arm. "You won't get away with this!" Marie snarled as she pushed her way inside. "I'll do whatever it takes to stop you."

18

"I don't know what you're talking about," Faith said as she stumbled backward. She tried to take comfort in the sight of the tiny dog in Marie's arms. *After all, what kind of killer would bring a poodle along to a murder?*

"Don't play dumb with me," Marie snapped. "I just had an extremely unpleasant conversation with a police officer. I know you're the one who sent him after me."

Faith stopped backing away and put her hands on her hips. She was growing tired of people accusing her of things. "I didn't send anyone after you. The Lighthouse Bay Police Department doesn't answer to me."

The other woman narrowed her eyes at Faith. "Someone sent them after me, and Caroline doesn't have that kind of courage. So that leaves you."

Honestly confused, Faith asked, "Why would you think Caroline could send the police after you?"

"She overheard a spat between Charles and me," Marie said. "Which you know full well. I've heard how you're poking your nose into the business of everyone in the society. Now you are just trying to distract me. You sent the police to my room."

Faith sighed. "Someone stuck the ace of spades on my door last night with a letter opener. When the police came to collect the card and letter opener, I mentioned that you'd been nervous about playing cards yesterday, which was true." Then she paused before adding, "And I did tell them about your argument. Caroline told me."

"As I thought." Marie peered around the room. "Where is your cat?"

Faith felt a rush of alarm. Surely she didn't intend to hurt Watson. "Why?"

"I would like to put Bijou on the floor, but if your cat is around, she will chase him."

"You can put Bijou down," Faith said, relief flooding her veins. "Watson is in the bedroom." As Marie put the little dog on the floor, Faith added, "I'm sorry if the police visit upset you, but you have nothing to worry about if you haven't done anything."

Marie's defiant stance suddenly melted away and she swayed a little. "You do not understand. I have done something."

As Marie's face paled, Faith reached out to catch her by the arm. She was concerned the woman might faint right in front of her. "Why don't you come and sit down? We can talk." Marie offered no resistance as Faith led her to one of the two chairs near the fireplace. "Can I get you something? A drink of water? Or coffee? I can put on water for tea if you like."

A weak smile barely lifted the corners of the woman's mouth. "Coffee would be nice. Black, please."

Faith poured Marie a cup and brought her own mug along as well. She sat in the other chair near the fireplace. "Why don't you tell me what's going on?"

Marie closed her eyes and took a long sip of her coffee. She met Faith's gaze and said, "I will tell you but it's a long story."

"I have time."

Marie took a deep breath. "I have always loved numbers. Since I was a little girl I have known I want a quiet life with numbers. But that is not what members of my family wanted." She stopped, shuddered, and took another sip of coffee.

"Your family?" Faith prompted.

Marie addressed her remarks to the dark liquid in her cup. "In France, my family is quite well-known. They operate all over the world."

Operate? What does that mean? Faith wanted to shake the woman to get her to spit out whatever she was hesitant to say, but she forced herself to sip her own coffee calmly and wait.

Marie wrapped both hands around the cup. Her gaze stayed fixed on the coffee, and she spoke without looking at Faith. "My family steals. They are mostly jewel thieves, but they are not exclusive. Whatever is valuable, they will take. They have been like this for generations."

Faith gasped softly. "*You* broke into the rooms."

Marie slowly raised her head, her eyes brimming with tears. "I did. I did not want to but I did. The only thing I have wanted in my life is to get away from the legacy of my family."

"Then why did you do it?"

Again, Marie's gaze turned back to her coffee. "Charles found out about my past. I do not know how. He and I have never gotten along. When I first joined the society, he treated me as he treats most women, but I told him that he was a pig. He never forgave that."

Charles hadn't struck Faith as the forgiving type. "He threatened you?"

"He said if I did not take the jewelry he would tell my employers about my family and that I was also a thief. I was trained to steal by my family, but that is not what I wanted. I fled France and came to America. I changed my name. I went to college. I like my life of numbers." Marie broke down and sobbed.

Faith retrieved a box of tissues for the distraught woman and waited until her weeping had softened into sniffs and gulps. Then she said, "You thought your employer would believe Charles?"

"I do not think so. But they would still fire me. I work for a large jewelry company. I only do their accounting, but they still could not employ someone thought to be a jewel thief. Believing me would not be the issue. Their image for their customers would be the issue. To stand by me would cost them too much."

"Why did Charles want you to steal jewelry?"

"You misunderstand. The jewelry was only a ruse, a way to cover up what he really wanted from those rooms."

"So what did he really want?"

"Information. He told me to take pictures of everything with writing on it. All papers. And I had to copy the hard drives of the laptops in each room. I did this, and then I took the jewelry, but I left the playing cards. I could have left the rooms without anyone knowing, but he said he wanted them to feel vulnerable. Charles commissioned that deck. I hoped someone would make the connection."

"You know this all sounds like a very good motive for murder."

Fresh tears filled Marie's eyes. "I know this. And I am not sorry Charles is dead. He was a terrible toad of a man, but I had no part in his death. I am not a violent woman. That is why I left my family."

"Leaving a playing card stabbed into my door is kind of violent," Faith accused.

"I did not leave that card. You can go through my deck, if you want. I have my ace of spades. I am only missing the two cards I left in the rooms when I took the jewelry."

"So you didn't put the ace in Walden's hat either?" Faith asked.

"No."

"How about the playing card torn up and left on Charles's body?"

"That also was not me. I told you, I only left the cards in the rooms I stole from."

Faith pondered the other woman's answers. Marie sounded sincere, but she certainly had a strong motive for murder. "Why did Charles want information about Evelyn Pugh and Morton Alried?"

"He never told me. I believe he wanted to do to them what he did to me—use the information to make them do as he said."

"But what could he want?"

"I do not know. He and Evelyn disagreed often about society business." Marie offered a small smile. "I think Evelyn disagreed with him simply for the pleasure of making him angry. But Morton was barely involved with society business. I do not think they ever fought, but I am not sure."

"Did you find anything worth blackmailing over?"

Marie shrugged. "Again, I do not know. The papers I found did not seem suspicious. Maybe there was something on the laptops? I did not have time to go through what I took from there. I do not know if Charles really expected to find anything. He hoped. He believed everyone has secrets. This is the way of truly bad men. They believe everyone else is also bad."

Faith settled back in her chair and thought about the things Marie had just said. A thought dawned on her. "Do you think blackmail could be the way Charles Huffam so often got the society to do what he wanted? Evelyn said she never understood why so many people voted for him to be president of the society."

"It is possible," Marie said. "I did not vote for Charles, but he did not have leverage over me then. I thought maybe he gave people money to vote for him." Then she looked down at her little dog on the floor at her feet. "Human beings are bewildering. This is why I prefer my Bijou. She and I understand each other. We are good to each other."

At the sound of her name, the poodle sat up and wagged her tail.

"I know this is not something you want to hear, but I think you need to tell the police all these things you have just told me. You did some bad things, but you were forced into them. Eventually they will figure out this stuff anyway, and it will be much better if you volunteer the information before that happens."

Marie's eyes filled with tears again, but she met Faith's gaze squarely. "I am not opposed to paying the price for what I did. I should never have stolen for that man. I should have taken a stand and let him tell my bosses about my past. But I am afraid they will think I am the killer of Charles Huffam and look no further. This would let a killer run free."

"They're certainly going to examine you pretty closely," Faith said. "But I meant what I said about the Lighthouse Bay Police Department. They are very good. They won't stop investigating just because you are a strong suspect." *I hope. Though that seems to be what they've done since they arrested Walden.*

Marie didn't answer right away. She sat quietly, appearing much smaller now as she huddled in her chair and stared down at her dog. "I will do as you say. I will tell the police what I did. But I need you to do something for me."

Faith realized Marie was probably going to ask her to take care of Bijou. She wondered if she'd be able to avoid World War III if she moved a dog into her cottage with Watson. Still, she did feel a certain amount of responsibility. If Marie came forward, she would be doing it because of Faith. With a sigh, Faith said, "What do you want me to do?"

"Promise me that you will continue searching for the killer and asking questions," Marie said earnestly. "I did not kill Charles. And I do not believe Walden did such a terrible thing either. But someone in the society is a killer. Please find that person."

"I'm neither a police officer nor a detective."

"No, but you are relentless. I can see this in your face. I feel certain that you will find the answer. If you say you will do this, I will go to the police."

Faith took a deep breath and felt as if she were diving from a terrifying place, but she kept her voice firm as she said, "I will keep looking. I don't know what I'll discover, but I won't quit until I find the answer or the police do."

She watched the other woman's shoulders relax. As Marie took another sip of her coffee, Faith hoped she could keep up her end of the deal. She would have to identify the real killer before the society all went their separate ways the next morning. If she didn't, Walden or Marie could go to prison for a murder neither one of them had committed.

19

"Shall I go now?" Marie asked. "I know you will be making a big leap of trust, but I will not run away from what I have done." She scooped up the poodle from the floor at her feet and held her out to Faith. "If you want, I will leave my Bijou as proof of my speaking the truth."

The woman's expression was so earnest that Faith suppressed the urge to giggle at the idea of holding a poodle for ransom. "I don't need to keep your dog. I believe you. But the sooner you go to the police, the better. You don't want them coming to you first, and they will."

"I will." Marie's face still had little color, but her jaw was set in determination.

As soon as Faith closed the door behind Marie and her little dog, she glanced up at the clock on the fireplace mantel. She needed to get moving if she was going to open the library on time. She rushed to her bedroom and nearly tripped over Watson, who raced by her as soon as she opened the door.

"It's too late," she called after him. "The poodle is gone. You can't terrorize her."

If Watson had a reply to that, Faith didn't hear it.

She quickly dressed in a long, soft alpaca wool skirt in a muted blue and a matching sweater. She gave her hair a quick brush and put on some light makeup, dabbing on a little extra concealer to cover up the dark circles from her nightmare-fueled night. Her cheeks were still pale, but time was passing quickly and it would have to do. "I'll fit right in with the Victorians," she said. "They admired ghastly pale women."

Watson absolutely refused to be left behind, nearly climbing onto the toes of her boots as she walked to the front door. She knew if she didn't take him, he'd just pull one of his stunts and end up at the manor anyway. Bending down, she picked him up and gave him a hug, despite his disgruntled refusal to snuggle. "You're a crab this morning," she scolded. "I didn't leave you in the bedroom *that* long."

When Faith got outside, she found the weather had warmed up considerably and melted away the snow. Now the ground was spongy under her boots and made soft squishing noises as she walked. "I hope this isn't a preview of Christmas," she told Watson. "Mom loves a white Christmas, not a soggy one."

Watson squirmed in her arms, so she gave in and set him down. He picked his way along the damp ground, an expression of utmost distaste on his face, but he refused when she offered to carry him again.

Stuffing her hands into her coat pockets, Faith quickened her pace so she'd get to the library on time. As she walked, her mind turned back to the murder. She now knew who had broken into the rooms at the manor and why, but did that get her any closer to identifying the killer? She didn't believe Marie had killed Charles. Faith had misjudged people in the past, but Marie seemed sincere. She admitted she wouldn't mourn Huffam, but she hadn't killed him.

Still, the whole reason Charles had sent Marie into the guest suites was because he was a serial blackmailer. He'd blackmailed Marie into stealing. Could blackmail be how he got to be president of the society? If that was the case, anyone who'd been blackmailed into voting for him had a motive for murder. *I certainly narrowed down the suspect pool.*

If it had been someone who'd been blackmailed in the past, why wait until now to kill Huffam? Bashing someone in the head with a length of chain suggested a crime of passion, so maybe it was someone he'd recently enraged. Evelyn or Morton, the society members he had robbed?

Evelyn certainly didn't seem to be driven by rage. She seemed to view most things connected to the society with a kind of amused cynicism.

But Faith knew a lot less about Morton. She'd had only one conversation with the man, which wasn't much to go on, but she had trouble seeing him as a murderer, even if he was angry. Though he'd appeared physically strong enough to wield the chain, he didn't seem to have the temperament to do such a thing. But now that she thought about it, his gentle shyness could be an act. It seemed many of the society members made a practice of concealing their true natures. As she turned the idea over and over in her head, she increasingly felt that the police ought to take a closer look at Morton.

Faith tried to remember what she had found out about Morton from her Internet search. He had basically been at the bottom of her suspect pool then, but she remembered that he was quite wealthy and on the board of several charities. Not that being charitable didn't mean he couldn't kill someone with enough provocation.

She was so caught up in her theories that she barely noticed she'd reached the manor until her boots were ringing against the marble floor of the main hall. As she turned and strode down the long gallery, with Watson at her side, her view of the library entrance was partially blocked by the statue of Agatha Christie and the small Christmas trees that surrounded it, each hung with miniature books, golden quill pens, and other book-related ornaments.

Someone waited at the library doors, but Faith couldn't recognize who it was. Glimpses through the Christmas trees suggested it was a man, and he wasn't wearing the uniform of the Lighthouse Bay Police Department. *So hopefully there's no fresh bad news.*

Watson paused to sniff around at the base of the trees, but Faith circled the display so she could reach the waiting patron. To her discomfort, she immediately recognized the man waiting by the library doors—Morton.

"I'm sorry to be here so early," he said shyly. "I know how annoying it is when you don't get a moment to gather yourself when you get to work, but I'm so eager to hear what you'd learned about the copy of *Great Expectations* that I borrowed." He stepped aside to make way for Faith to unlock the library door.

"No problem," Faith said faintly, uncomfortable with the coincidence of finding him at the library door right after she'd been debating the odds of him being a killer. What if he somehow read her suspicions on her face? She wasn't certain it was a good idea to be alone in the library with him now that she knew he might have been a target of Charles's blackmail and had reason to want him dead, but she couldn't exactly bar a guest from the library. He had a legitimate reason for coming in. So she fumbled for the keys and unlocked the library door.

The staff had already been in, and a cheerful fire burned in the big library fireplace. "I do have some information about the book," she said, distressed to find her voice sounded shaky.

"I'm so glad. Was it Martita Hunt?" His eyes were bright and his voice eager, but she still couldn't tell his true intentions.

"It was," Faith said. "And the Wilfred was Wilfred Jaxon, the current Mr. Jaxon's grandfather. He met the actress when he was in California. He was considering investing in a movie."

"Did they have a romantic connection?" he asked.

"Apparently not," Faith said. "Or if he did, his grandson didn't know about it."

"Maybe it was a secret romance. Thank you so much for checking into it for me. I'm glad to hear the story. I don't suppose I could purchase the book?"

"I'm sorry, no," Faith said. "The book has strong ties to Jaxon family history, so it will have to stay in the library collection."

"I understand. I would have loved to add it to my own collection, but I cannot blame Mr. Jaxon for wishing to keep it in his."

Since Morton seemed so calm, Faith decided to probe him for information. She didn't dare launch into questions about the murder directly, but she could steer the conversation around to the burglary to see if she could learn anything from him. "I'm glad I was able to find out about the inscription for you. And I hope you've been able to enjoy your stay here overall. Especially in light of the awful burglaries and, of course, Mr. Huffam's death."

He waved the comment away. "I'm just grateful the police found my cuff link collection. It has been passed down in the family for three generations. I heard from the chief this morning. He assured me they would take excellent care of my property and return it as soon as possible."

"It must have been very upsetting when they were stolen."

"It certainly didn't please me. I have them insured, thank goodness. I honestly am not that particular about my cuff links, but they reflect family history. The collection originally belonged to my grandfather. I value them for that, which is why I understand the Jaxons valuing that book."

"Why do you think Mr. Huffam would steal your collection?" she asked, keeping her voice as light as possible. "He didn't seem to be lacking money."

"That's not what I heard," Morton said. "In fact, one of the companies I am associated with—a publishing conglomerate—was considering buying Huffam Publishing. The final vote on the buy is coming up, though I'm certain the vote and the sale will be postponed as his estate is dealt with."

Faith felt a tingle of interest. Could this be related to the murder? "How did Mr. Huffam feel about selling his publishing company?"

"I honestly don't know. Good, I imagine. It wasn't a hostile takeover by any means, and it would inject a great deal of money and clout into his company. The likelihood is that he could have still run Huffam Publishing if he wanted."

"How sure was the sale?"

"A few of us on the board were mildly hesitant. Huffam Publishing has an impressive history and a good reputation, but I've been less than impressed with where the company has gone in the last decade." He smiled. "Here I am, blabbing away. Surely you're not really interested in all this talk about publishing companies."

"I *am* a librarian," Faith said, "so anything connected with books interests me. I normally don't deal with books until the end of the process, but the publishing industry is fascinating."

Morton chuckled. "I don't often hear a pretty young woman call my work fascinating."

"Of course it is, if only because it reminds me how small the world really is. For example, if you were involved with the purchase, you must have worked closely with Mr. Huffam. I love finding little connections like that."

He shook his head. "I was really just a vote on a board. The rest of the board listens to me, don't get me wrong, but I didn't have a tremendously strong feeling either way about the purchase. And I didn't know Charles all that well. I rather disapproved of the way he behaved around some of our female members, but he certainly seemed committed to being society president."

"Did he talk to you about the purchase during the gala?"

"He tried on the first day, but that's not why I come to society functions, so I asked him not to bring it up again. I wanted to get away from work for a few days and disappear into the world of Charles Dickens. I admire the works of Dickens so much, which is one more reason I am grateful for the time you spent tracking down that inscription."

"I was happy to do it," Faith said. "I have to admit your finding it made me curious as well."

"History does that to me, particularly the history of a book. Tell me, Miss Newberry, will you be attending the society's ball tonight?"

"I will. Mr. Jaxon will be there, and I am attending with him."

"Will you really?" The delight that lit his face seemed to strip years from him. "The two of you will make a handsome couple."

She laughed. "I suspect you're a romantic, Mr. Alried."

"Guilty as charged. I'll look for you at the ball. Perhaps you'll even save me a dance?"

"I could probably manage that," Faith said, responding to his smile in spite of herself. Then the corners of her lips fell as she realized their conversation had not brought her one iota further along in her investigation. How was she ever going to find Charles's killer at this rate?

After thanking her again, Morton spotted Watson and bent to scratch him on the head. "Is this your cat, or is he the library cat?"

"I suppose he's both now," Faith said. "I can't manage to keep him at home. But Watson and I have been together for nearly fourteen years now."

"I had a Jack Russell terrier for about that long," he said. "I miss him every day. The only sad thing about pets is they can't stay with us for our lifetime."

"That's very true," Faith said, feeling a tug of sympathy for the man. As much as Watson drove her to distraction sometimes, she couldn't imagine being without him.

"Well, I will see you tonight." With another of his gentle smiles, Morton took his leave.

The quiet man had barely exited the library when Evelyn swept in, carrying her calico cat in her arms. "My darling Little Nell absolutely insisted on coming with me. I think she knew I would be seeing her boyfriend," she said as she put the Manx cat on the floor.

Little Nell immediately raced over to Watson and began licking his face.

"I decided to risk bringing her despite all the dogs around. She's actually the braver of my two darlings. Dora is positively frantic over dogs."

"I'm sure Watson is happy to see her," Faith lied. She could tell by Watson's tense pose and flattened ears that he was less than thrilled with Little Nell's enthusiastic affection. She hoped he wouldn't become annoyed enough to scratch, though she wondered if even that would dampen the Manx's ardor. "Did you come by just to play matchmaker or do you need a librarian?"

"Neither," Evelyn said brightly. "I thought you might like to join me for lunch in my suite again. There are so few truly interesting people to chat with here. I've known all the society members for so long. Plus, my girls always adore a visit from Watson."

"I would certainly love lunching with you, but I should probably eat at my desk today. I have to check in all the outstanding library books and get the library ready for our Christmas break."

Evelyn put out her lip. "I'm horribly disappointed but I'll be brave about it. Are you going to the ball tonight? Perhaps we can chat then."

"I am," Faith said. "Though I'm not at all used to such an elaborate or closely fitted gown as I'll be wearing, so you may find me in the corner trying to breathe."

Evelyn laughed. "Breathlessness is one of the biggest Victorian challenges."

Before either of them could say anything else, loud footsteps drew their attention to the library door. Octavia burst in, her gaze sweeping sharply over the huge library before landing on Faith. She pointed a long, bony finger in Faith's direction. "You! I know what you're trying to do."

"Me?" Faith squeaked.

"Caroline told me about your *sleuthing*." She made the word sound distinctly unsavory. "You better mind your own business if you know what's good for you!"

And with that she whirled around and stomped back out.

Faith watched her go in stunned silence, mentally moving Octavia to the top of her suspect list.

20

The final borrowed library book came back well before lunch, and Faith was able to do all the last-minute chores needed to close up the library. She'd still have to pop in briefly in the morning, but she might actually get to Springfield by lunchtime tomorrow instead of after dark. Her mom would love that. She considered calling Evelyn to see if she wanted to have lunch with her after all but decided it was too late for such a request to be polite.

"Well, Watson, nothing left to do but worry," she said.

Watson tilted his head as she spoke, as if trying to work out the whole concept of worrying.

Faith chuckled. "I know. Life is simple when you're a cat. 'Where's my lunch? Where should I nap next? What's this in my fur?' I really don't know how you manage."

Watson yawned widely, showing off his small sharp teeth and pink tongue. Then he settled down on the desk and blinked sleepy eyes at her.

"Don't fall asleep. We're going home." She scooped him up and closed the library.

Once she got to the cottage, she realized she felt as much at loose ends at home as she did at the library. Faith wrapped the last of her presents and took the ball gown out of the garment bag to hang it for a while before dressing. As she admired the faintly shimmering fabric of the gown, a knot of panic formed in her stomach. What if she was clumsy and hopeless in such a big dress?

In the kitchen, she fixed a cup of hot tea and sat down at the table with her laptop. Faith thought about Octavia's threatening attitude earlier. How much did she really know about her? She quickly found the same links she'd followed before, the ones that identified Octavia as the widow of an influential man and a retired school principal who spent most of her time involved in Charles Dickens Society events.

She studied some photos of Octavia. In a few of them Caroline lurked in the background, but whenever she was with her mother, Octavia dominated the scene. Faith was a little surprised that a woman who seemed so devoted to the society and so intent on getting attention didn't hold a current office. She could be unpleasant, but that was true of Charles as well. Then again, it was beginning to look like Charles had blackmailed his way into office. Maybe Octavia didn't have that kind of leverage. Or maybe she'd held office in the past and now wanted to focus on her imagined romance with Charles.

Though Faith dug deeper and deeper, she wasn't able to uncover anything worrisome in Octavia's background. She found plenty of references to Octavia online, but nothing seemed scandalous or suggestive of a propensity for violence. Faith tried to picture the older woman wielding a length of chain against a tall man like Charles and discovered that her imagination didn't stretch that far. Still, she knew people were capable of amazing things when angry, and Octavia had been furious over Charles's remarks to Faith.

"You were a woman scorned," Faith murmured to the picture of Octavia on her screen. "But did your fury turn into murder?"

She picked up her cup of tea and found the last sip cold. She noticed the clock on her laptop screen and gulped. It was past time to start getting ready, especially since she still had no idea what to do with her hair.

After a couple of hours spent trying every hairstyle she could imagine and even a few that she found on the Internet, she ran out of time and dressed. Faith had settled on pulling her hair up on the back of her head and securing it with every hairpin she owned, leaving a spill of curls on each side. She tucked two gold combs into her hair as her only ornamentation and hoped it would do.

She'd just snatched her keys off the table in the kitchen when she realized she had no idea how she'd cram all of her skirt into her Honda and still have enough room to drive. "Fine, I'll walk." She headed back to the bedroom to change her shoes for some heeled boots that would make walking a little easier.

Her winter coat closed at the top, but she had to leave all the lower buttons open since it wasn't designed for wearing over a Victorian gown. "How did women ever get out of the house?" she complained as she wrestled with the coat.

Watson watched her preparations with more interest than he usually showed in her clothing efforts. He seemed especially fascinated by the swish of the long skirt near the floor.

Faith pointed at him when he lunged for the ruffle at the bottom of the dress. "Leave that alone. Iris just fixed it. And don't get any ideas about coming with me. You're staying home where it's warm and dry."

As she walked through the dark gardens toward the manor, Faith began to relax despite the chill breeze. The simple act of holding up her skirts made her feel a bit like a character in a Victorian novel, though she was sure carrying the shoes she intended to dance in qualified as some kind of faux pas. She realized she was eager to try dancing in the dress after all, or at least she was eager to see the society members sweeping around the ballroom as the hired orchestra played.

Nearing the manor, she spotted movement on the terrace outside the library, so she detoured to walk the steps up to the terrace to see who might be out there. She found Caroline pacing across the tiles. "Isn't it a little chilly for strolling the terrace tonight?" Faith asked, keeping her voice intentionally light.

The corners of Caroline's mouth turned up, though her lips trembled and the smile didn't reach her eyes. "I'm trying to walk off some of my nerves."

"Are you worried about Mr. Garder?"

"Yes, but not exactly the way you mean." Caroline took a deep breath. "The police released him. They didn't have enough evidence for an arrest, and they won't because Walden certainly didn't kill anyone." She paused, then blurted, "Walden and I have decided to announce our engagement. He's wanted to for months, but I have only just realized how important it is to seize the time we have." Wringing her hands, she seemed to vibrate with worry. "Mother will be furious."

"She might be," Faith agreed, "but she isn't the one getting married. You're a grown adult, and you should be free to make your own decisions."

"I know. I know. But it isn't easy. The last time I made a decision Mother didn't like, she worked herself up into some kind of attack and landed in the hospital. How do I live with that kind of guilt?"

"By realizing that it's not your fault. You don't control your mother. And she only controls you if you let her."

Caroline's face brightened. "You're right. Walden says the same things. You're both right." She stood up straight. "I have to be brave. She chooses her own reactions, not me."

"Would you like me to walk in with you?"

Caroline's eyes widened. "Would you? I somehow feel braver around you. You always seem so sure of yourself."

Faith almost laughed at that, but she didn't want to undermine Caroline's fragile confidence. Together they walked around the terrace to the front of the house and entered through the vestibule.

Although most of the guests mingled in the Great Hall where the orchestra was warming up, Faith spotted Walden lurking just inside the doorway. He seemed to catch sight of them at the same time and rushed in their direction. He caught hold of Caroline's hands. "You disappeared on me. I've been so worried."

"I needed a little fresh air." Caroline beamed into Walden's face. "Shall we go and visit the refreshment table? I could use some wassail."

His concern melted into a matching smile. "Yes, let's."

After a little finger wave at Faith, Caroline slipped her hand through the crook of Walden's arm, and they strolled away.

Faith felt a warm glow as she watched them. She hoped they'd have a happy Christmas after all.

"Faith!" She turned her head to see Wolfe walking in from the gallery. "You look lovely. Are you ready for a real Victorian ball?"

"I'm not sure. I've never danced in a dress like this one, so I'll apologize in advance if I end up on your toes."

"I'll take the risk." He offered her his arm. "Shall we?"

Paved with marble squares like the gallery, the two-story Great Hall never failed to impress, but the room seemed especially magnificent to Faith as she gazed around in delight. It sparkled with tiny white lights and gilt Christmas decorations, which seemed the ideal accompaniment to the colorful gowns of the society women.

"It's all so beautiful," Faith said.

"I agree," Wolfe said. "Before we start dancing, can I get you some punch? I'm told the kitchen has prepared a delicious one."

"Thank you," Faith said.

As Wolfe strode across the hall, Faith enjoyed the chance to watch him from a distance. The cut of his suit perfectly matched both the Victorian theme and his tall, athletic build. She jumped as someone laid a hand on her arm.

"So our handsome host is your date?" Evelyn said, eyes sparkling with mischief. "Lucky girl."

"It's a work event," Faith said for the umpteenth time. Since she had no interest in discussing her love life or lack thereof with Evelyn, she quickly changed the subject and complimented the other woman's rich burgundy velvet gown. "Did it come from the boutique?"

"With as many society events as I attend, I've built up quite a wardrobe. Can I steal you away? There's something I want to show you about the case. It's a clue I discovered, but I want to show you in private."

Faith glanced back toward the refreshment table but couldn't spot Wolfe through the crowd. Surely he would forgive her for slipping away. "Will it take long? I don't want to leave my boss alone."

"I doubt Wolfe Jaxon spends much time alone," Evelyn said. "I assure you I'll have you back before any of the society women move in on him."

She tugged on Faith's arm, and Faith followed her across the hall and through corridors and passages until they weren't far from the pet spa, which was closed for the night. "Where exactly is this clue you want me to see? We can't get much more private without going outside."

"I agree. This seems far enough." Evelyn reached into the beaded bag she carried and pulled out a gun. To Faith's horror, she pointed it directly at her. "I'm terribly sorry. I really am. I like you, but I do need to get this settled before we leave tomorrow."

"I don't understand."

"Come on, dear, think about it. You're bright."

It clicked and Faith gasped. "*You* killed Charles."

Evelyn smiled like an aunt whose niece had just figured out something incredibly difficult. "I knew you'd get it. I did. You see, he discovered something about me when he burgled my room—something rather unfortunate."

"And he blackmailed you," Faith said, careful not to show the fear that threatened to overwhelm her. "It must have been bad if you killed him over it."

Evelyn sighed. "Yes, it was. My late husband died of . . . unnatural causes, but I was the only one who knew it. Until Charles found out. And now you. It's freeing to talk about it, but it requires such strenuous cleanup effort afterward."

"You murdered your own husband?"

"Don't look so shocked. He was an odious man. Impossible to be in the same room with for any length of time. His only good point was his wealth, and I kept that. I assure you, no one wept over the passing of Augustus Pugh. And aside from Octavia's crocodile tears, no one wept for Charles."

"And no one will weep for me?"

"I am sorry I have to kill you. Yours is the only death I will mourn. We could have been such good friends if you hadn't been so clever. Maybe I'll adopt dear Watson as a memorial to you."

"But why kill me? I never suspected you. You could have gotten away with it." With a sinking heart, Faith recognized that this might be true. Evelyn could have been gone tomorrow, and no one would have been the wiser. Was there any chance someone would venture down this hallway?

"Because you won't leave things alone. The police seemed content to dig away in entirely the wrong direction, but you kept picking and picking, even after my ketchup-covered letter opener and my aces of spades. I thought I'd made it plenty clear, but now I realize I will have to be blunt. The investigation is over."

"You think shooting me will end the investigation? Walden Garder's been released," Faith said, her voice climbing as adrenaline rushed through her veins. "The police know somebody killed Charles—they'll start taking a closer look at everyone here—including you." *I have to stall for time. Someone will come out here sooner or later. Please let it be sooner.* "And they *will* track down who killed him—and me. I have friends and family who won't allow them to let it go."

"Of that, I have no doubt. And I hope they do. It'll be thrilling to watch your boss rush around trying to bring you postmortem justice." Evelyn waved the gun. "That's why I picked this. It belongs to Octavia. Thankfully it's all registered and legal. All I have to do is wipe it down and leave it in her room when I'm done with this distasteful business. Maybe I'll even plant it on her. She'll be the perfect villain. She threatened you right in front of me today. I was so horrified by the encounter that I spent almost all day telling people about it. So the police will track down the gun and hear about Octavia's threats, and the whole case will be over."

Faith realized the plan sounded far more realistic than she liked. "You really believe they'll accept Octavia as Charles's killer? She loved him."

"That's one of the best reasons to kill. She was a twisted, hateful, jealous woman, and she saw Charles make a pass at you, as well as plenty of other women. Add in your encouraging Caroline's defiance of her mother for trying to run her life and your own nosy ways, and everyone will believe she killed you. No one will even question it." Evelyn's expression turned grim and she lifted the gun, holding it in two hands as she pointed it at Faith. The barrel of the gun might as well have been a cannon. "Good-bye, my dear. I do hope you understand it's nothing personal."

"No!" Octavia screamed and burst from the shadows near the end of the hall. She charged at Evelyn and hurled herself on the other woman before Evelyn could turn around in her heavy skirts.

Faith grabbed one of the heavy plaster dog statues from the alcove next to the pet spa. She rushed to the struggling women, reaching them just as the gun went off.

Octavia crumpled to the floor.

Faith raised the dog statue and bashed Evelyn's arm before she could turn to face her again. Evelyn cried out and dropped the gun. Faith and Evelyn scrambled for the fallen gun, but they were both badly hampered by the vast skirts of their ball gowns. The gun disappeared and reappeared in their sweeping skirts over and over as they snatched at it.

Faith managed to grab the gun. She jumped back, stumbling over her dress, and trained the gun on Evelyn. "Don't move," she ordered, panting.

The sound of the gun going off must have carried because soon the corridor filled with curious guests.

"Help!" Faith yelled. "Octavia Skimsby has been shot!"

Luckily the society included one doctor, who was able to stanch Octavia's bleeding while they waited for an ambulance.

Faith was hugely relieved to hand the gun over as soon as the manor security arrived. They could watch over Evelyn until the police arrived.

Wolfe coaxed the rest of the guests out of the hall and away from the spilled blood, though the ball was clearly over. He returned to stand with Faith as the police arrived to take Evelyn into custody. Faith paid little attention as she prayed softly under her breath for Octavia. In spite of all her bitterness, anger, delusions, and manipulation, the older woman had saved Faith's life.

"Miss Newberry?" Chief Garris said. "We'll need a statement."

"Can she come by in the morning and give it?" Wolfe asked. "I think Faith has been through enough tonight."

"That should be fine."

Faith didn't even mind them making the decision for her. She felt numb with worry.

As the ambulance attendants loaded Octavia onto a stretcher under the watchful eye of Caroline and the society doctor, Faith walked over to her. "You saved my life."

Octavia attempted an imperious sniff, but it turned into a soft gasp. "I wasn't going to let that woman frame me for murder. It had nothing to do with you."

"Still," Faith said, "I'm grateful."

"We're ready to go," the ambulance attendant said.

"Hold on," Octavia said. She turned to Caroline. "You best bring Walden to the hospital with you, since I'll need to get used to him."

Caroline's face blossomed into a smile, and she squeezed her mother's hand. "Do you mean that?"

"Of course. Despite what that horrible murdering woman said, I am not trying to run your life. You love him. You should have him. I do want you to be happy."

The glow on Caroline's face as she followed the stretcher down the hall was almost enough to make up for the horrible evening. Faith shuddered. *Almost.*

Wolfe placed a hand in the center of Faith's back and gently ushered her out of the crime scene. When they reached the Great Hall, they saw that most of the guests had left the room, probably to head up to bed or congregate elsewhere to talk about what had just happened. Faith couldn't blame them. She was ready for this awful night to be over.

Wolfe and Faith watched the orchestra quietly packing up to leave. Faith felt a well of disappointment in her chest. She was glad to have found the killer, but now she'd never find out what it would feel like to dance with her handsome boss. She looked at him. "Are you leaving for Europe tomorrow?"

"I have an early flight. Are you leaving for home in the morning?"

"Late morning," she agreed. "I have a few things to finish up in the library. Then I have to go by my aunt Eileen's to reassure her about a fish."

"Your aunt keeps fish?"

"No, the fish is for my father."

"Your father keeps fish?"

"Only briefly." At Wolfe's confused face, Faith suppressed a laugh. "My dad loves to fish so my aunt knit him a sweater with a fish on it. I have to pass judgment on whether it's an acceptable fish."

"Well, naturally."

Faith wondered if someone so immaculate in his clothing choices would ever consider wearing a sweater with a smirking fish on it. Though she doubted it, she enjoyed imagining Wolfe in a sweater exactly like that, and she giggled involuntarily.

He raised an eyebrow. "Something amuses you?"

"Eileen tells me it's rather funny," she said. Then she sighed. "I'm probably just a little punchy from leftover adrenaline. It's been a challenging week."

"It has," he agreed.

They watched the orchestra again for a while before Wolfe added, "You know, I'm very disappointed that I didn't get to dance with you tonight."

"After wrestling Evelyn in this dress, I'm not sure whether I could dance in it or simply trip and stumble in time to the music. But it might have been fun to try."

"That sounds like an experiment we need to do," Wolfe said firmly. He crossed the rest of the distance to the orchestra.

The orchestra leader looked down at Wolfe from the raised platform they were on, and Wolfe gestured him over. After they exchanged whispered conversation, the leader gave the orchestra an order Faith couldn't quite hear. The musicians unpacked again and set up while Faith watched, her stomach knotting with nerves or excitement or—more likely—a mixture of both.

Wolfe walked back to stand in front of Faith. He bowed deeply, then gestured toward the orchestra, which began to play.

Wolfe held out his hand. "May I have this dance, Miss Newberry?"

Faith offered him a curtsy. "I would be honored, Mr. Jaxon." She put her hand in his. His arm circled her waist, and they swept around the room in a perfect waltz.

As the music and Wolfe carried her along, Faith found that she wouldn't mind if the night lasted a little longer after all.